THE SPECIAL FRUIT COMPANY

THOMAS TIMMINS

THE SPECIAL FRUIT COMPANY

Book two of

THE HOUR BETWEEN ONE AND TWO

A mystery in three books

THOMAS TIMMINS

Zoëtown Media
Haydenville, Massachusetts

ZOËTOWN MEDIA

The Special Fruit Company
Copyright © 2014 by Thomas Timmins

Cover: Tom Dudley

Zoëtown Media ISBN: 978-0-9893283-1-9

Printed in the United States of America

Disclaimer

The author admits to taking a decade-long trip through the humid world of tofu making and marketing. He met countless inspired, industrious, good and eccentric people as he and his cohorts transformed soybeans into food for human beings. While some may wish to attribute familiar identities to some of the characters, living or dead, this is not a memoir. It is a work of fiction, arising from the author's imagination. Like all tall tales, it has at best a metaphoric relationship with what we perceive as the everyday world. If you find truth and pleasure in this book, they are yours to enjoy. That would make the author happy as the tofu master who, after stirring endless circles in a cauldron of hot soymilk, whips up a tasty batch of tofu he can serve to the world.

ACKNOWLEDGEMENTS:

Joe Timmins, David Grant, Angela Borda, Nancy Shobe, Barbara Sachs, Judith Rubenstein, Amy Swisher, Thomas Dudley all had sensitive and caring hands in the making of this book. Without Judith Roberts, Richard and Kathy Leviton, Madeleine Fox, Jon Lee, Vinny Natale, Maggie Stebbins, Cory Greenberg, Donnie Nelson, Mary Houghton and hundreds of crew members and thousands of imaginative and intrepid tofu aficionados, the author could never have made the astonishing journey from soybean slinger to tofu tale teller. I thank each one of you.

Contents

Prologue

Genevieve

Tofu:
It's What You Make Of It

A Cookbook by
Genevieve Mellon O'Connor & friends

Dedication

Every recipe in this book came from a woman of the land, beginning with Amanda Ralston of Taugatuck, New York. I'd been taking photographs of wild flowers, got lost on a country road, and had a blowout at dusk. No cell phone reception, on the verge of panic. An old pickup with dim lights approached and stopped. A small woman, dressed like she just came from church, jumped out of the truck, fixed the flat, and invited me to her farm home for tea.

Well, tea turned into a long gab about food, children, families, men, art, and more food. When I told her my job was Vice President of Marketing for a tofu company, she laughed and said, "You're having dinner with us." In half an hour, she served me and her family their favorite tofu recipe: meatballs. Who'd have thought a livestock farmer from the backcountry would know about tofu?

Over dessert, we concocted the idea of a cookbook based on tofu recipes from the farms and villages and cities of America named Tofu: It's What You Make Of It. Some food marketing people are saying we've abandoned the cooking culture and joined the eating culture. My friends and I say, who's going to cook what you eat?

On my web site, you can read the life stories and see my photo portraits of my creative new friends from all across the country: From Eveline Jessup in Pine Valley, Georgia, to Betty Ann Fettig in Milford, Iowa, to Juanita Gomez in Salinas, California, thank you to the most capable women I've ever met.

This book is dedicated to all of you beautiful, ingenious, soulful women of the land, whether you live in the country or the city. You've taken your salt-of-the-earth way of life and spiced up bland old tofu into succulent dishes no hungry man, woman, or child could ever resist.

From the Introduction to:
Tofu: It's What You Make of It
Genevieve Mellon O'Connor
American Tofu, Inc., Clement, New York
www.AmericanTofu.com

Chapter One

Genevieve O'Connor

A CAREER CHANGE

By Thanksgiving of the year I joined American Tofu, my ten-year old son Liam and I were down to our last four hundred dollars. The job at the newspaper had ended when the owner's hand strayed one time too often.

I'd come to Clement the spring before because I needed a change from my old life on Cape Cod. *Winny's of Wellfleet*, my best friend's art gallery that I'd managed for five years, was closing its doors for good in March. Jason, the man who came closest to being the love of my life, left me six months earlier. I spent endless hours sitting in front of my fireplace during the lonely, barren winter, dreaming about our future, wondering what I had to do to make sure Liam had everything he needed.

Liam and I would need a bigger place soon. He needed a lot more space at home than I could give him in our one and a half bedroom apartment. But if I gave it up, I doubted that I could find an affordable year-round apartment, or, dream of dreams, a house anywhere I'd want to live on the Cape.

We moved to P-town when Liam was two. He loved the town, the people, his friends. He swam and sailed every summer and played hockey on the ponds in winter. My friends had become our family. Liam had more women uncles and men aunts than any other child I knew.

My life there had been great for seven years. When Jason split, he took my enthusiasm for P-town life with him. If *Winny's* had stayed open, maybe I'd have postponed our leaving, maybe not. If I was going, Liam was at the perfect age to make a school change, before the cliques started forming in middle school and while he was still too young to feel I'd ruin his life by forcing him to leave his friends.

I told Winny I planned to leave Provincetown.

"It's time, Winny. I can't hang around P-town forever waiting for my boat to come in. I need to try something different. Besides, Liam needs to go be a teenager in a regular town."

"Makes me too sad, Hon. I'll miss you too much."

Tears came to his eyes. I started crying and leaned into him.

"Liam in a normal town? He'll be so bored. God, G, we'd take a lot better care of Liam's manhood in P-town than those manipulative little girls and those violent little boys out there in that decadent straight world. Not to mention those slimy pedophiles sneaking around."

I laughed. He hugged me.

"You? You're another story. I love you and want you to have the maximum best this life can give you."

Whatever my motives for leaving, Winny was my friend. He persuaded his uncle in the rural upstate New York town of Clement to hire me as graphics manager for his newspaper.

"It's beautiful in upstate New York, honey," Winny said. "If you want normal, Clement's middle name is 'Boresville.' I should know. I lived there sixteen lonely years before I got the guts to let my high school drama teacher take me to the city. I never looked back."

"I could use small town boredom for a while, Winny. I'll meet somebody."

"You always do."

Winny took both my hands and put them to his cheeks. "My advice, little sis? Come back here by next summer."

I ignored Winny's pessimism. He didn't want to lose us, but I was determined to make it work out in Clement.

***

After two months in my new town, I lost the newspaper job, my first straight job in years.

When Winny's brainless and resolutely heterosexual uncle's hand brushed my breasts the second time—the first I'd let go as his clumsiness—I erased the day's advertising layout five minutes before deadline and walked out. Standing in front of the newspaper office that afternoon, all I wanted was to get in my car, pick up Liam, and flee to the Cape.

Instead, I drove to the park at the edge of town and sobbed. I had no friends, no love, and now, no job.

The inland skies over Clement barely glowed. The thin light sunk into the earth, clutched it like a fearful mother, spreading a greenish shadow over everything.

I couldn't let myself fall into self-pity. I told myself I just needed time to establish a stable life for Liam and time to find some new friends for myself.

Liam and I decided to rent a house at the lake for the summer. We'd keep our apartment in town, but spend most days and nights at the lake. We'd garden, swim, sail, and plan our next move. I calculated that my savings would last until at least the end of the year when I'd have to find a job. We moved to a three-room cabin on the lake with a view through oaks and cottonwoods out over placid blue water.

Liam said, "Mom, I'm glad we're here. We have to recharge our batteries. I like Clement, but sometimes I feel lonely. It'll take us a while to settle in. I'm sure when school starts up I'll make lots of friends."

I didn't know whether I should be grateful for having such a wise son, or sad because he'd grown up so fast and shouldn't really know his mother so well.

I'm not complaining. I'd never complain about Liam and me. Moan and groan, a little, that's healthy enough. I'm just so deeply in love with my son, it scares me. Not in any bizarre incestuous way, just a pure love that colors every corner of my life and sings to me when I'm hurting. I joy in my mothering of Liam. A lot of times I think, I don't matter, except for Liam—that scares me, too.

Still, I can't imagine a life with any less love. It's odd, backwards, somehow, but I feel this total freedom that comes from my mother love. I've never felt that kind of freedom with a man, maybe because I've never surrendered to a man the way I give in, in my bones, to mothering.

If I ever met a man who makes me feel even freer, even more myself, he's the one who will sweep me away. The one time since Liam was born the right man came close, he split. I've come to wonder if I'm too much for a man. Too independent, too free, too much a mother.

When we came to Clement, I put my desire for a man on the back burner. We'd come for Liam's teenage years, and I'd still be in my thirties when he left for college. That gave me plenty of time to meet somebody.

Maybe living in Clement, without a man calling every day, wouldn't get lonely, but I doubted that. All my life, I'd kept some relationship simmering, if for nothing more than to keep myself company. The way I could keep myself from rushing into something with a man was to accept loneliness as a regular visitor. It would be good for my character, but terrible for my sex life.

Liam and I enjoyed the lake so much that the summer disappeared before I'd had a chance to find a steady income. We rented a sailboat and sailed every day. In rain, we rowed across the lake, unless we heard thunder. I met plenty of single fathers of his lake friends and uncles and married dads' best buddies. I went out every week, but not one interested me enough to have dinner with him a second time.

***

Once we came back from the lake in time for school, I looked seriously for a job, never expecting how hard it would be. The possibility I'd end up clerking in a grocery store, office temping, pizza delivering, or night managing the downtown McDonald's depressed me enough that I almost called the jerk at the newspaper and asked for my job back.

A job managing the local frame shop and art supply store opened up in mid-November. It paid barely enough to cover our rent and food, but I needed to find something before the snow fell. They offered me the job, and I said I'd let them know after Thanksgiving.

Then I met Nora at the Salvation Army Thanksgiving Day dinner where Liam and I had volunteered to help serve the needy.

Nora was friendlier than the average Clem citizen, and she took a liking to Liam, praising him for his generosity and civic sense. Of course, he had no idea what she was talking about. As far as he knew, we were simply doing what we always did on Thanksgiving. We'd started serving up spuds and breasts at the "Salvo" five years before in Wellfleet when we had no place else to celebrate Turkey Day.

Nora was petite, raven-haired, shapely, pretty but not striking. Her face was kind, totally wrinkle-free, she looked thirty. She dressed conservatively but expensively, though you probably couldn't tell unless you knew fabric as I did. Her two most arresting features were her slightly bulging royal blue eyes that looked at you as if you were the most important person in the world. And she listened like a born therapist. When she told me that she was six years older than me, I complimented her on her complexion. She claimed it was her vegetarian diet that kept her looking so young.

As she scooped potatoes, I sliced and forked out the white meat. Liam stood proudly at the end of the table, waving his spatula and talking non-stop as he served the apple and pumpkin pies.

Usually I'm reserved with new people. In Clement, where everyone knew everyone else, reserve was a survival tactic for a single woman. But with Nora, in between filling plates and joking with the diners, I jabbered on about my money situation, my newspaper boss's fondling, my fears for Liam, my artist's life on the Cape.

She told me that she painted and asked me to look at her work sometime.

"Maybe you can you tell me if it's worth trying to sell."

"It's always worth trying," I said. "I don't have to see it to say that. I don't know if I can tell you, but I'd like to see your work. It can be great and not sell."

I was starving for the company of artistic spirits. She was the first artist I'd met since I left the Cape.

She pulled me away from the table as soon as the last guest had received her turkey and gravy. I told Liam to go ahead and sit down to eat, I'd be right back. He'd met some new kids, so while he enjoyed his first Thanksgiving away from Massachusetts, Nora and I sat in the chaplain's office and I told an abbreviated version of my life's story.

When I finished, she took my hand and said, "Go see my husband Monday. We have a food company and he needs a salesperson desperately. You'd be perfect, Genevieve."

My heart leapt, but I doubted the job was for me.

"I've never sold anything but art," I said.

She grinned. "Hey, if you can sell art, selling tofu's gonna be a piece of cake...tofu cheesecake." She laughed and stood up. "Let's go have our pumpkin pie. I'll tell Charlie all about you. Really. Call him."

She didn't worry about my looks, so I assumed she had a solid marriage. I hoped we would become friends. I needed a good friend.

Chapter Two

Charlie Greer

A GOURMET COOK

silver earrings, green eyes
she laughs, who could resist?
the tofu spring starts in December

"What d'you know about tofu?" I asked Genevieve O'Connor the afternoon we met almost two years before Becky MacDaniel died. "Or soybeans? Health food?"

Glancing at her résumé, I said, "Art major. Photographer. Worked in a gallery? Ever do any food photography? By the way," I said, softening my tone, "call me Charlie."

I didn't mean to confront her. When I get nervous, words flood out of my mouth. She should have been the nervous one but women like her always agitate me, especially when I'm not expecting them.

Before she walked into my office, I'd imagined an attractive and personable woman who, according to my wife, Nora, was someone who "...could help us with sales." Instead, a lovely, elegant woman sat across from me, smiling as calmly as a lioness playing with her game.

Get control, Greer. You're the boss here.

Jiminy, my inner fool. Nothing I can do about him. p"To tell the truth?" Genevieve said, showing me her sparkling teeth. "I don't know much except a few recipes I took out of magazines. Tofu's a cheese made from soybeans?"

She paused, expecting me to answer. I sat there, saying her name to myself. Genevieve. She pronounced it the French way. I said it to myself. *Zhon a vee ev. Zhon a vee ev.* Too many syllables. Thought I might as well call her Gen.

"No cholesterol. Low fat. Stops hot flashes?" she asked. "Reduces the risk of cancer in women. Men, too. The Chinese invented it thousands of years ago, right? Most Americans still don't know how to use it, do they?"

She'd done her homework. A natural sales woman, she drew me in with her questions, then she made the irresistible offer.

"I'm a good cook. Italian. Chinese. Japanese. Couple of Thai dishes everyone raves about. I'm really good at making up recipes."

She laughed nonchalantly as if she'd let me in on an embarrassing family secret. I'm a picky eater but I was already eager to taste any new dish she felt like trying out on me.

"I'll make up some tofu recipes for you. I may not be much of a salesman," she said, the two words "salesman" stressed ironically, in good humor. "I wasn't a great photographer when I started out, either."

She combed her fingers through her hair while she spoke. When people fidget, it usually means they're uncomfortable. With Genevieve, I let the gentle raking motion mesmerize me.

"At the least, Charlie, you need me for my cooking."

I needed her for some other things, too. Not for what I thought, as it turned out but, right then, I just wanted her.

Jiminy jumped into my thoughts.

Your little brain's running the tofu train.

"I may not know much about health food or soybeans," she slowed her pacing, "but I know people."

Crossing her legs, she sat back with her hands in her lap.

"I bet I can read your mind right now."

She showed me the widest smile I'd ever seen in my office.

"I'm not going to say what you're thinking."

She knew. How could I think anything else? Was she flirting or challenging? Genevieve Mellon O'Connor. Long russet hair tinged with gold flowed over the shoulders of a rich brown business suit. Her green eyes had crinkles at the corners that revealed warmth. Her eyes held mine, inviting me to search them. Silver spirals dangled from her ears gracing a sensual neck.

While she talked, I examined her. I pretended that I was a supermarket buyer observing this tall, attractive woman who wanted to sell me a low profit item. I noticed that her teeth weren't perfectly straight. They were white as a TV toothpaste model's, though. While I loved her free-flowing hair, it could use brushing or a permanent before she tried to sell anyone tofu. She had no pretentions. She was a regular guy, who happened to be a woman. As a buyer, I liked what I saw.

My observation skills had improved dramatically since I started writing haiku. It's what you have to do when you practice haiku. Basho, the ancient Japanese haiku master, teaches that truth lies in beauty seen up close. Now I can see beauty everywhere. Strange thing, since I started writing haiku, business started getting better.

"More than anything," Genevieve said, speaking in a low pitch that forced me to lean toward her to hear, "I know people. Isn't that what you really need, Charlie? Don't worry about me and the customers. I tell it like it is. I handle myself. I'm used to guys acting idiotic when they see me. I'm pretty, but not sensational, thank God. What is it? My mother gave me her spirit. I love life. I love people. I'm not afraid. Everybody likes people who love life."

I nodded. She was smart. I like intelligent women, especially if they're working for me. Genevieve sounded like she'd thought about things. Maybe I'd learn from her.

Most of what I know about life I've learned from women. I'd have to teach her about business, though.

"One thing you don't have to worry about? I don't believe in sexual harassment. I'm always in control. If I see a problem coming, I take care of it before it gets out of hand."

Where did that come from? Sexual harassment made me nervous.

Reading my mind again, she said, "It came up at my last job. He was a jerk who didn't know any better."

Her candor began to convince me she was strong enough to handle the job, because we both knew that plenty of guys would come on to her and there was nothing I could do to make it easier on her. Then she clinched it. Nora would insist I hire her when she heard what she said next.

"I'm a feminist. I have high standards. I expect to be treated respectfully."

As if waiting for me to acknowledge her conditions, she stopped speaking, raised her eyebrows and held my look.

"Of course," I said. "I respect every woman. I'm the son of a woman. I have a wife I love and respect. I have little daughter who deserves only love and respect. I'll do anything I can to make sure she gets it."

Genevieve smiled and nodded.

"You're really going to like having me around, don't you think?"

She was right, of course. I loved having her around. She not only sold more tofu in two years than any other Caucasian, living or dead, but with her brains and guts, she saved me and my family from ruin.

"You act like I made up my mind," I said, wiping any expression from my face, invoking my position as president.

"Well, haven't you?"

"Maybe," I said, grinning, reassuming my authority. "We do need people who know people. But can you sell? You've mostly worked in galleries."

Genevieve smiled. I had the oddest feeling high in my chest. A knob of energy rose into my throat that only a growl would relieve. I felt like I was back in my college fraternity again, stupid with testosterone. I began to inhale in rapid short sniffs.

Of course, Jiminy sounded off.

She's blasting you with pheromones. Stand up. Walk around. Open the window. She's gonna give you more grief than you've ever had in your life.

Jiminy always snapped at me whenever I acted the slightest bit irrational. Under the pretense of acting like my conscience, it tried to make me guilty just for throwing myself into life's possibilities.

"I'm thirty-two and I've been around. Had a lot of different jobs. I know, you can't ask me how old I am, but I can tell you. My mother died when I was twelve and I had to take care of my dad. He was a drunk. Died a few years ago. My husband left me when I was pregnant. I get zero child support and for 11 years, I've raised Liam by myself. We've never been hungry. Don't you think I can handle a little tofu?"

"What about pay?"

Enjoying her personal disclosures, sympathizing with a tough life that assured me she could handle the job, I admitted to myself that I'd hired her.

"Pay me what you'd pay any sales manager. I'm not worried. We need health insurance."

It was simple. If she sold our customers half as easily as she sold me, she'd make me king of tofu before she was through. We decided that she would start the next week. When I saw a rusty Subaru parked in front of the building, I realized I'd need to get her a car. The job called for a lot of road work.

She was a survivor, a mother, not a career path woman. I'd known a few other single mothers who had created wildly successful careers for themselves because they were motivated by their kids. It's what's called intrinsic motivation. When I hire men, I look for their I. M. that makes them want to be heroes.

Nora and I preferred to hire family people. Well, she preferred it and I did it. It all worked out because they're like us, Nora said, family. They needed jobs and they'd stick with us. We're one big family.

Instead of a family, I saw us at best as a clan. If we're a family, you can't get rid of anyone, and I've had to fire my share.

Genevieve apologized for not being used to dressing up every day to impress customers.

"Don't worry," I said, pulling up the company checkbook on the computer and printing out an advance. I took the sheet out of the printer, signed it, handed it to her.

"Three thousand dollars!"

"I know how much women's clothes cost. You should see Nora's charge card at Lord and Taylor's."

"Charlie, I can't take this. There's no way I can pay you back." "Take it. If things work out, it's an investment. If not? Well...I know you'll try as hard as you can."

She wavered. I knew she didn't want to feel indebted to me. She was too independent.

"I see it as a signing bonus. You're going to bring it back into the company in the form of a classy image and big sales. Image is what sells, you know."

She finally relented and we shook hands warmly, congratulating each other on our mutual decision. I hired her because she had desire, and she needed the job. Not to mention my desire, of a different kind, which compelled me to make a decision I'd never regret.

Some people, women usually, say that men make all their decisions with their gonads. That may be true, even unfortunate in some cases. But I say that I've made many of my best decisions because I followed the guidance of those smart fellas down below. "Los cojones" the guys in the factory say.

As she was leaving, I suggested that she read up on Chinese New Year, the best time of year to make big tofu sales. When I told her the Year of the Sheep was coming up, she laughed.

"I used to spin wool," she said, "when I lived on a farm in Connecticut.

Curious to learn as much as I could about this fascinating woman, yet not wishing to act too eager, I said, "Oh yeah?"

"Living the simple life when my son was born," she said. "It's different now. Thanks a lot, Charlie. See you soon."

We shook hands again and she clicked my office door shut behind her.

I pumped my fist into the air, whirled around, and started talking to myself. "Way to go, Greer. You lucky dog. You must be doing something right. Jee-sus! They'll never stop you now!"

Smirking to myself like a fool, I collapsed into my leather president's chair and tilted back, clenching my hands in glee. Three thousand dollars was a big advance, especially when we had ten thousand in the checkbook in those days, but true entrepreneurs know when to leap.

I knew Genevieve O'Connor was worth the risk. We needed the sales, bad. I'd just ordered state-of-the-art manufacturing equipment from Japan that we had to have, but I didn't know how we were going to pay for it. I had the feeling that Genevieve was the key to taking American Tofu up to the next level. I couldn't wait to unleash her on my customers. Big time, here we come.

Chapter Three

Genevieve O'Connor

"YUCK!"

The afternoon I left Charlie Greer's office I felt as elated as I'd felt since I left Provincetown.

I'd told him enough so he could convince himself he'd made a rational decision. He had that same look in his eyes every man has when he gets my full attention, the look that says I want you, I'll do anything to have you. I saw that he'd made up his mind to hire me the minute we met. I was the one who had to make the decision. He knew that, too.

I'm glad I did. Selling tofu wasn't my first choice of a job—nothing against tofu—I'd rather give food away. But I didn't have a choice right then.

Since I took the job, my life has never been richer, more filled with love, or more thrilling. Without the job, I'd be in some dead end relationship with a hardware store manager, living in a drafty old house on the edge of town, worrying about Liam using drugs because he couldn't find anything else to do in Clem.

Charlie is a decent man. He gave me the job and he came through in the end. He impressed me that first day when he said he gave 5% of his profits to hunger relief. He was handsome, younger-looking than his mid-forties. About my height, on the thin side, thick hair slicked up over his big head. A diamond stud in one ear. He'll never make GQ, but he's got a modern cool business image and a genuine smile. His best feature is that he comes across as sincere.

He'd decorated his office with a New Age mix of traditional oriental and high tech furnishings. We sat on a low couch, drinking herbal tea from heavy 50's-vintage white porcelain coffee mugs. I commented on the old blue and gray rug at our feet.

"It's authentic Chinese, maybe 200 years old. I found it in a garage sale in Rochester," he said.

A Japanese scroll painting with a mist-seeping-through-bamboo motif hung down one wall. Across from it and behind us, an iridescent velvet rendering of a fierce green and yellow dragon peered into the room. I almost asked him if he found it in a Chinatown bar, but when Charlie rubbed the dragon's nose, saying "My protector," I admired it.

A screensaver flock of white cubes with flapping wings drifted across a computer monitor sitting on his stainless steel and glass desk. I assumed it was tofu flying through the night. Flute music played while we talked.

"Classical bamboo," Charlie said when I asked him about it. "Might be from the Shang dynasty. Thousands of years ago."

When I noted the three avocado plants growing in red lacquered urns, he said, "I ate the fruit, sprouted the seed, cultured 'em myself. Three good friends. Mr Meng, Mr. Giordano, and Mr. MacKay. Our three best customers."

He laughed at my surprise.

"No, you don't have to shake hands. They remind me who pays the bills is all."

When I told Charlie how old I was, he flipped through a calendar with Chinese script on the cover.

"So, you're a Sheep. I should have known."

According to Chinese astrology, everybody born the same year as me was a Sheep. I mentioned my regular sign, Taurus, but he wasn't interested.

"Sheep and cows," he said. "Same thing to the Chinese. I worry a little bit about you as a sales manager. Sheep are compassionate, artistic, and peace-loving."

"That's me," I admitted.

"Can you handle the Tofu Wars?" he said. "Maybe you're a Wolf in Sheep's clothing."

He laughed. Charlie loves his own jokes.

He wanted me to ask him so I said, "What year were you born in?"

"I'm a Tiger. Tigers and Sheep work well together. My fearlessness and strength coupled with your artistry and care for people? We'll be unbeatable."

Even if Charlie'd been a jerk, I would have had to take the job. I knew he'd fall in love with me. Thank goodness, he was sweet. I planned to give him plenty of respect and appreciation. He not only expected it, he needed it. He was the kind of man who'd compete with me to give me even more esteem than I showed him, to show his superiority. Anyway, I always give more than I receive. You can never lose that way. That's why I became the best tofu salesman he ever had.

***

The money Charlie gave me the first day we met helped more than he could know. It went for winter coats and boots for Liam and me and two months' back rent. Even though I'm sure he would have let us, I couldn't ask Mr. Donahue to go another month without paying.

I dragged out some of the clothes I took home from Provincetown modeling jobs I did years ago. My figure had filled out some, but most of the clothes fit. I lowered and raised hems, sewed on a few buttons to some bright cotton blouses and polished a couple of pairs of heels. I created a wardrobe Charlie'd think I bought at Taylor's. I took my five chic gallery dresses and reworked them into a fashionable business wardrobe. I always buy quality and I stick with my colors year after year. Class and style survive the trends.

After my interview with Charlie, when I told Liam I'd taken a job selling tofu, he scrunched up his face and said, "Yuck!"

As usual, I told him I was glad he told me his true feelings, but he'd get used to tofu. I reminded him how he used to hate mushrooms until I sauteed them in butter and drizzled maple syrup over them.

"You can be my inspiration," I said. "I'll come up with some tofu recipes you won't be able to resist."

"Wanna bet?"

Chapter Four

Genevieve

WE SELL U 4 LESS

During my first two years at American Tofu, we more than doubled sales. Tofu was still the butt of a hundred jokes in the media and in the produce business. My standard was "Why did a tofu cross the road? To prove he wasn't a chicken."

I knew we had a real company as far as supermarket buyers were concerned when five different buyers told me the same crude risqué joke. "How are tofu and dildos alike? They're both meat substitutes." None of them looked me in the eye when they told the joke, but I laughed it off like one of the guys. From then on, they'd buy as much American Tofu as they could possibly sell.

I'd made new friends across the Northeast, driven 60,000 miles, and seen Liam grow into an independent middle-schooler. He still loved to snuggle with his mom while watching a movie and gobbling popcorn. It helped that I let him stir chocolate chips into the buttery, salty, soggy mass.

Nora and I had become close. She sometimes told me things about Charlie I didn't need to hear, like how lately he'd become cold in bed. He said it was because he was so worn out from working so much. But Nora said she needed a man in her bed, not a lump of tofu. She proceeded to get herself into trouble with her painting instructor, until Charlie found out and drove him out of town. I didn't really like being her marriage confidant, so I convinced them both to find a therapist. For the last few months, they've had the added pressure of the murder investigation, but they seem to be doing much better.

When our sometimes beloved, sometimes moronic, always charming CEO Charlie Greer traveled to Taiwan last month, we were all glad to get him out of sight. We had a lot of work to do in planning our next Chinese New Year of the Rooster sales promotion and Charlie's trip gave us the time we'd need to concentrate. This would be the biggest sales event we'd ever seen, and I had three people's work to handle. Mine, mine, and mine.

Jet lag must have worn Charlie out because when he returned, he seemed distracted, but he didn't say much about the trip other than Taiwan was crowded and polluted. He promised to show slides, but he never did. All he wanted to talk about was "Soy to the World."

He intended to design a logo and copyright the words then sell them to every soy farmer and company in the U.S. as well as across the globe. These new customers—"allies" Charlie called them would use the phrase and the image on their packages, their web sites, their trucks.

"Intellectual property, Gen. It's where the real value of a company is. Anybody can make tofu, but once we've copyrighted Soy to the World, we have something nobody has, nowhere. And they have to pay us to use it. Royalties."

We humored him because he became so wrapped up in his campaign that he left us alone to get our jobs done. I congratulated him on his fabulous idea but I wouldn't promise that I had time to help, at least until after the Year of the Rooster promotion.

"Wait till you read the article I wrote about my Taiwan trip. It'll be in all the trade journals—it's the next step in our STW promotion."

Charlie eventually told me about his escapade in the "barbershop." He lowered his voice, almost whispering, confessing.

"The girls were sex slaves," he said. "And Meng—he imports snake livers and dried deer penises and ground monkey balls and other aphrodisiacs."

I wasn't surprised. The Chinese diet contained all kinds of herbs and animal parts.

"He smuggles tea and who knows what all. Chinese restaurant workers? Chinatown sweatshop employees? I hope he's not into guns or drugs."

***

A couple of weeks after Charlie returned to the States, Meng called me asking if I could visit him the next time I came to New York. Meng's account was Charlie's responsibility, so I asked Meng if he wanted me to have Charlie come, too.

"No, just you, Ms. O'Connor. Please let me tell Charlie about my invitation. He's nervous about things right now and I'd like to tell him a little later."

Red alert. I'd tell Charlie right away. I wondered what Charlie had done in Taiwan to warrant a secret meeting with the Dragon of Hunts Point. Meng might be pulling me into the murky side of business way over my head.

"I wonder if you'd prefer to meet in the city? I know an excellent restaurant. Do you know the 'Adam's Rib' at the Palace?"

I almost dropped the phone. I blurted out "I'd rather meet at your place...office, I mean. It's easier."

I'd heard about the way the Chinese negotiate in the business world. They let you know your vulnerabilities right away. You know they'll do anything they have to to win your concession. During our affair, Gianni and I had made Adam's Rib our favorite restaurant and the Palace our regular hotel.

Worried about Meng's call, I rushed into Charlie's office and told him, expecting him to know what it was about.

"No idea, Gen. He's got something up his sleeve. Setting something up. Let's learn from his technique. Those Chinese know how to negotiate."

"He's your customer, Charlie. Why don't you handle it?" I didn't tell him Meng had mentioned the Palace and what that might mean. "He's giving you a big honor. They call it 'face.'"

Everybody knew about 'face.' Charlie talked about it every time he had a difficult conversation with anyone. Lately, he'd bragged how well he'd given the Chief 'face' and in return, he expected the investigation to wrap up any time.

"Tell you what. I'll go to Hunts Point with you. I'll drive so you can take a break. I'll wait for you across the Market at Giordano's."

Of course I knew where Giordano's office was even if I'd avoided it for the past few months, when Gianni was in town. I didn't want to see him but Charlie didn't need to know that. As it turned out, Gianni's schedule sent him out of town that morning but he invited Charlie to wait in his office.

"I'm on auto-pilot for you, Genevieve," he said when I called him. "Just tell me where you want me to touch down."

***

At dawn in the South Bronx, the first week of November, Charlie and I, in his midnight blue Beemer, followed a tractor-trailer emblazoned with the mud-spattered slogan "We Sell U 4 Less" toward the Hunts Point Produce Market. He pointed at the sign and groaned.

I laughed. "New York humor."

"Or bad translation," he said.

We stopped at a red light beside the truck and I snapped a photo for my collection of truck ads. The ten foot tall fence that ran beside the road had collected hundreds of plastic bags in its cross hatches. They glowed pink and lemon and gray as a light breeze inflated them like giant mushroom caps.

Charlie nodded absently as he stared out the windshield. When I saw what he saw, I said, "Poor things."

Two women, one lustrous brown, one white and deathly anemic, both wearing blonde wigs and brown trench coats and stiletto heels, stood on the curb in the mustard glow of a street light. Timing their move to our stopping, they pulled their coats open, revealing thin naked bodies. Both had ample breasts with long nipples and scrawny legs. They rolled their hips languidly. The white one stuck out a long pink tongue and wiggled it at me. They must have been so high they couldn't feel the cold on their skin. According to the car's thermometer, it was thirty-five degrees outside.

Last week it was seventy three in Clement and next week it could climb to eighty. At least with global warming, the girls of Hunts Point won't have to freeze when they show their bodies.

Charlie accelerated through the red light before they could approach the car.

"I forgot about this," he said. "Sorry."

I swung around to watch the whores. They seemed miserable. I faced forward and said, "No. I feel sorry for them. They're not dangerous. They're sisters. What's horrible is they're already good as dead."

Using my zoom, I made a portrait of the women through the car's back window. My camera kept me company on most of my sales trips and I often made portraits of the buyers and framed them for their homes or offices. They loved that. I'd keep these shots for my personal collection: "Travels for Tofu."

We rode toward the Market's main gate in silence. Every now and then Charlie glanced into his rear view mirror.

"A van stopped. One of them's getting in," he said.

"Forget them, Charlie. Let's go," I said. "I want to get off the street." Charlie gunned the accelerator and we left the women behind. We both needed to change the mood.

"Know what, boss?" I said. "I'm eager to meet Meng. I'm curious. Besides, I like foreign men."

"I know that," he chuckled. "But I don't think Meng's your type."

I laughed. "Boss is always right."

Charlie showed his pass at the gate and we cruised into the Market, entering a maze of warehouses and loading docks, heading for Aisle B-28 where the specialty produce companies had assigned berths.

We sold American Tofu to Giordano Brothers and Meng Produce and to their peers in produce distribution centers throughout the country from New York to Chicago, from Maine to Miami, from here to Los Angeles. Montreal and Vancouver were our only international markets, but Mexico City was on our radar.

Our distributors sold and delivered the tofu, along with their other produce items, to supermarkets, delis, corner stores, institutions like schools and hospitals. Some sold to the military, others made it available to health food stores. Sometimes, depending on the wishes of the supermarket chain, we sold our products directly to the retailer, avoiding the distributors.

Passing by a small warehouse that sold a little of our tofu, Charlie said, "That's where we can get those esoteric ingredients for the gourmet spaghetti sauce you told me about."

"Which one?"

"You know, the one you seduced Giordano with." Charlie couldn't resist ribbing me about Gianni. "You know you'd never have beaten me in the sales contest last year if you hadn't, you know, with Giordano."

"How many times do I have to tell you, it was not about that? Sales was a whole separate thing. Gianni doesn't make buying decisions—he runs the company." I should never have told Charlie.

"Whoever runs the company makes the buying decisions," Charlie said.

"Not at Giordano Brothers. Not even at AT. You don't make many buying decisions and you run the company."

"Still, if I was a single man and had a woman business associate hot for me, my sales would go one way: up."

"Forget it, Charlie. Just be happy you have such a successful business."

"You're right. It doesn't matter how we got there—the end justifies the mean. Machiavelli. Italian, right? Knew all about how people use their ends to get what they want. Just like any other primate. Sex."

"Shut up, Charlie. Don't be mean."

"I'm sorry. Just teasing."

For all his so-called wit, Charlie could get tiresome. He drove fast and we bounced over the potholes, rocking us from side to side and back and forth, in silence.

Charlie parked under a bare incandescent bulb the size of a gourd, the only light that shone among a dozen empty sockets at the end of the dock. We got out and veered across the greasy parking lot, avoiding puddles and slippery gray leaves and smashed brown pulp. I could see tiny movements out of the corners of my eyes.

"I hate rats," I said, clutching his coat sleeve.

"Keep moving. They'll stay in hiding."

I hoped they would. I remembered the doubts I had when I first came to the pre-dawn Market's filthy alleys crowded with idling trucks and shouting men. Now it felt as familiar and safe as a college campus. I knew dozens of guys here who'd take care of me if any little thing happened.

Behind us, a caravan of empty trailers rumbled and boomed as the tractors, belching diesel fumes, bounced from bump to pothole to bump in the access road between warehouses. Coughing, we ran to escape the slime the truck tires splashed everywhere. I still gripped Charlie's arm as we trekked between rows of parked tractor-trailers and climbed a set of rickety stairs.

Harsh voices and loud laughs echoed off the metal warehouse walls. A sour fermented smell dosed the air. Standing on the loading dock, I said, "It doesn't smell as bad as it does in the summer, like a dumpster behind a restaurant. But there's some perfume in the air, too. It's kind of rosy."

"You have a good nose," Charlie said. "Too cold for my sniffer. I can't smell the flower market and it's only in the next lane over, but you're right. In July, this place stinks like a dump."

"Let's go to Blooms 'n All after my meeting," I said. "Bring some flowers back to the office to celebrate. I'm going to have a great meeting, Charlie. I can feel it."

"Positive affirmation, Gen. Proud of you. Only way to go."

Geez, Charlie, I thought. You think everybody's your kid.

As we walked down the cement platform leading to Giordano's, men appeared wide-eyed from the backs of the long-haul rigs. The workers stopped and called my name. Truck loaders in parkas burst out from between the wide plastic strips that curtained the warehouse door. Drivers leapt the stairs two at a time from the parking lot below.

I felt like a long lost queen returning to her castle. As we reached the Giordano crew, at least a dozen men in heavy coats and dirty aprons circled around us.

"Where you been, Genny-vee-ev? We missed you."

"Hi, guys." The last time I was here I'd bought breakfast for everyone. I was so distracted by Meng I forgot to buy even bagels or donuts.

"Come to get me for brunch?" another called out.

"I been savin' that Chianti I told you about. How 'bout comin' over after work?" That was gray-haired, sunburned Rico, my favorite.

I laughed. "Sure. What time will that be?"

The rest of the crew started pummeling Rico. He lit up and said, "You like fusilli or rigatoni with your lamb?"

"Whatever you want, sweetie. It's your party."

Everyone laughed. The men invited themselves to the party and five offered to drive me to Rico's house.

"You'll have to pick me up in Clement," I said. "Gotta see my son first."

"I'll pick you up in Roma," Rico said. Someone else hollered, "That's nothin'. I'll pick you up in a limo." Another guy climbed up on a box and threw his hands into the air. "Hey, Genny-vee-ev, get this. I'll rent a helichopper."

"Better start saving your pennies, Gary. You know what a chopper costs?" He shrugged.

"You show up in a helicopter, and I'll take the ride," I said, lifting my hand in a salute.

All the men started shouting and snapping their aprons at each other until a short young man in a Mets stocking cap hollered, "All right. All right. Cool it. Get back to work. She's here to see the boss." Nobody moved but they quieted down.

"Thank you, Donello. You know I don't mind the guys. They're sweet." I tilted my head and said, "Charlie. Remember him?" They glanced at him. "He's my boss. Gonna wait for me in Mr. Giordano's office while I go to a meeting over at the competition."

"You goin' to the Chink's?"

"Meng Produce, Bobby. Another customer," I said, maintaining my neutrality. Every ethnic company feigned hate for every other, though after work, you'd find Chinese, Salvadorans, Koreans, Italians, Croatians, Puerto Ricans, Australians, Africans, nearly every other nationality or race of men drinking together in the local bars.

"We'll take care of your boss, Genny. You just say the word."

I loved my produce warehouse guys. They made me feel like I was the only woman in the world, and in their world of trucks and boxes, I usually was. I believed they'd do just about anything for me, if I asked.

I shook hands with the men, high-fiving some, trying to remember all their names, giggling when I got it right. All the attention made me feel giddy, almost tipsy, even if it was just fooling around.

"Sell a lot of tofu!" I called as Charlie and I turned to enter the warehouse.

All the men smiled and one said, "Hey, Genny-vee-ev. Don't worry. We'll sell tofu to Donello's grandma."

Everyone laughed. "Yeah. Right."

"You d'Man, Donello."

Someone whined, "Charlie, Charlie." He turned back. "Tell me what to do, boss," the man said, kneeling down with his hands pressed in prayer. "I got a problem with somethin' beautiful."

Charlie and I laughed with them, then slipped through the plastic strip curtain hanging over the twenty-foot wide ten-foot tall doorway.

"Don't worry, Charlie," I said as we climbed the metal stairs to the main office. He followed me, pretending to shield me from the workmen's hungry eyes. "They treat me like a sister."

"If that's how brothers treat you," Charlie said, "no wonder there's a taboo against incest."

Once we entered the cool, spicy order of the warehouse, all traces of the Market's squalor disappeared. Pallets piled high with common vegetables and fruits in boxes arranged in clean, precise rows stood ready to salute.

Ugli fruits, miniature bananas, pink tangerines, white papayas, marbled grapes, mushrooms labeled with oriental script, yellow thorny vegetables, and other nameless stars of haute cuisine all waited under fluorescent lights for their chances to audition on the fine china of white table restaurants around the city. Racks of pallets lined the walls thirty feet high, holding white pails of olives, silver tins of nut butters, crimson and brass buckets filled with olive and sesame oils, and transparent five-gallon carafes of imported vinegars.

Charlie picked up one of the fruits. "Think you could make up some recipes for tofu using Ugli fruit?"

I thought a moment. "Would you really want people saying tofu and Ugli fruit in the same breath?"

"Mmm. Yeah. Didn't think about that."

"What about a salad with tofu, grapes and toasted walnuts and a tart dressing with balsamic, light on the olive oil, heavy on the garlic?"

Impressed, Charlie said, "I'd try that."

The temperature in the warehouse felt the same as outside. The whole room was a vast refrigerator. Its forty-foot ceilings extended so far back from the loading dock that we couldn't see the rear wall.

The scene moved me so much, a warm shiver passed down my back. Surrounding us was a testament to the global village. The food came from all parts of the planet. The hooded faces of Giordano employees who moved briskly around the warehouse riding electric pallet jacks, hauling boxes, shouting to each other, came in all the human colors and sizes, black, yellow, brown, white. I heard five different languages spoken as we headed toward the stairs.

I watched, amazed that our little tofus had entered the vast river of calories that flowed ceaselessly through Hunts Point out into the insatiable alimentary systems of New York.

"Awesome," I said.

"Yeah. I get a buzz every time I see this." Charlie twirled in a circle, his arm up, fingers giving a palms-up blessing to the foods. "This is why we're in the food business. Everybody's gotta eat. American Tofu is the healthiest food anyone can eat."

We climbed three flights of stairs to the office level. We knocked and Gianni's assistant opened the door, inviting us into the office. We stepped onto the bridge of a yacht. The window wrapped around the room, halfway down all four walls. The view out the back window wall over the roofs of the Market toward the Bronx on one side and the Manhattan skyline on the other made me imagine I was powering down the Harlem River, heading for sea. The entire front wall was glass through which he could watch his warehouse crew at work.

Across the carpeted office, an oval conference table gleamed under shaded wall lamps. Between the table and us, a leather couch and three chairs surrounded a lacquered coffee table. The contrast between the rubbishy Market streets outside and the Park Avenue elegance of his office always fascinated me.

"Not bad," Charlie said. "Someday I'll have an office like this."

We sat at a small table as a young man in a white coat and black pants served us. Sipping cappuccino and nibbling biscotti in silence, we watched the sun wash the shadows down Manhattan's eager skyscrapers.

"You better go," Charlie said. "Don't keep Meng waiting." "Charlie, will you relax?"

"I can't. You know I can't, ever since Becky died. The Chief's snooping everywhere. I know that's what Meng wants to talk about."

"Take it easy. I thought you gave him so much face the only place he'll want to snoop is in the mirror." Charlie groaned. "Have a cappuccino and enjoy the view. I'll be back and we'll go buy some flowers and have a nice lunch. Want to go to Cuchi Fritos? Plantains and fried chicken. You can't do anything right now, so just sit here and accept it."

"Easy for you to say."

Charlie stood up to help me put my coat on. "Good luck." He hugged me. "Watch for any weird products at Meng's."

His face was gray and his normally trim suit was wrinkled. "Like what?"

"Snakes. Dried deer penises. Rhino horns. Like that."

"Sure thing, Charlie. I'll brush up on my Chinese on the way over."

He stared at me.

"To read the labels," I said.

***

"Hello, Mr. Meng," I said as he rose from his massive black lacquered desk. I always called him "Mr. Meng."

Not only was he nearly a foot shorter than me, but he wore a five-thousand dollar silk suit that glowed with midnight iridescence, and a diamond as big as my thumbnail adorned his little finger. As imposing as he was, despite his tiny stature, what made me most cautious was I'd entered an alien world populated by powerful men who experienced the world in ways that I would never understand.

I'd never seen a woman other than me in his warehouse, not even in the administrative office, and I assumed that everyone, except maybe Charlie, in his stubborn democratic naiveté, paid Meng a lord's deference.

In his office, Meng expected and received my complete attention and formal respect. We sat on low ivory stools at a small jade table inlaid with scenes of farmers and crops, hunters and animals, fishermen and fish.

"Fifteenth century." He nodded casually at the table and stools I was staring at. "They have more sentimental than economic value. We trace the group back to an ancestor thirty-four generations past. As you can see, it foreshadowed our interest in the food business."

I shifted on the stool like many uncomfortable servants of the Empire called to meet at this table during the last five hundred years.

He poured tea into tiny cups painted with ornate calligraphy. He said the tea set, while not really a unique work of art, also had some sentimental value because it had been in his family for ten generations.

"I enjoy serving tea, Ms. O'Connor, especially to Americans. It gives you time to slow down and relax. You all work too hard. It's something I have learned from my Japanese associates."

My eyes scanned the room and landed on a long mahogany bar next his desk. In the shadows above the bar, thick shelves carried an exhibit of whiskey bottles any four-star bar would be proud of.

He noticed my glance lingering on the bottles. "Would you prefer a whiskey instead, Ms. O'Connor? Powers Gold? Ireland's finest."

"No, thank you."

"A liqueur? Midori? Campari and soda? My daughter tells me it's her favorite."

"No, Mr. Meng. Really. I don't drink. It's kind of you, but I prefer the tea." I picked up my cup and had a tiny sip. A little smoky, spicy. "Delicious."

He asked me about my family, my background. When I told him about my previous career as a gallery manager and a photographer, he asked me to sit beside him on the couch. He showed me a fat album of family snapshots. His two sons lived in Taiwan where they ran an import-export business. Meng had dozens of photos of his grandchildren.

He smiled as he turned the pages to a series dedicated to his daughter. "She is something like you, my Shu Ling. An artist. She wants to make movies." He pointed to a broad-faced, grinning girl dressed in a white evening gown.

She was a cold and arrogant rich kid, as far as I was concerned. She'd all but ignored me while she made her film of AT. She had Charlie following her around, wagging his tail and panting like a lost puppy. Everybody in the plant made jokes about him and his 'Tokyo Rose' behind his back.

"I met her at the tofu plant. She seems very smart and competent. We're excited about the film."

"I'm proud of her," he said, "but I am not sure what will become of her. She's our 'untamed mare.' She's determined to stay in the States. She's still quite young, though she imagines she's a woman of the world."

Meng began our formal meeting, first moving us to comfortable chairs and pouring more tea. "I appreciate all you have done to increase our tofu sales, Ms. O'Connor. You have also improved sales of some of our other products."

"Thank you, Mr. Meng. Please call me Genevieve. Everybody does." I gazed down into his face, noting that he didn't resent my superior height in my heels. I wore them on purpose, a demonstration for Meng of my professional persona. "Your success is my success," I smiled. "Without you, we would have much less success."

He returned my smile and, holding my eyes, poured more tea. We drank without speaking, listening to the muffled racket of empty trucks careening and jangling down the pot-holed passages between the warehouses. I felt as relaxed as a mouse in a cheese barn, sensing the cat close by.

"A very nice tofu firm from Canada has approached me," he continued. "They call themselves 'U.S. Tofu.' Do you think that's strange?"

I agreed it was. I sipped tea and ventured, "It could even be a trademark infringement," offering him resistance and intelligence in the same breath.

I recalled one of the sales seminars Charlie had sent me to. I'd use its strategy for dealing with Meng, like I did with other men customers.

If you mirror their self-importance, they'll never know it but they'll think you're the same as them. Let them wonder later why they respect you so much.

Placing his cup on the table beside his chair, Meng smiled and went on. "The company is a division of a large dairy and marine enterprise. The son of the owner runs the tofu operation. He wants to enter this market very badly."

I settled back, but held his eye as he launched into a little lecture.

"We're now riding a wave of Asian products entering the U.S. market. The farms are finally large enough to supply an export market. From bok choy to schizandra, the supermarkets will never be the same. Even your Mr. Giordano has made a great deal of money from Oriental products. However, I don't carry Italian or even Belgian products in my warehouse."

Concealing my discomfort, I decided I'd better deflect the conversation away from references to "my" Mr. Giordano toward the business at hand.

"Mr. Meng, Charlie really should know about this."

"He knows about it, Genevieve." He pronounced my name hurriedly, as if he wanted to brush it off his lips. "I called him a few minutes before you arrived to let him know you were coming to see me. I also told him about U.S. Tofu. More tea?"

Cringing at Meng's attempt to undermine Charlie's trust in me and make me an unwitting player in some game he had going with Charlie, I set my jaw and accepted the tea. As he poured, he said "I had the feeling he knew about our meeting before I called him today."

Of course Charlie betrayed my confiding in him about the meeting. He had to let Meng know who was in control of me. Boys.

Holding the warm teapot between his palms, then setting it down beside his empty cup, Meng stood up, gracefully, but abruptly ending the meeting before I touched my freshened cup.

"I told Charlie that if any new developments happened before I saw you, I'd give you the update on the situation. He hopes you can discuss this with Mr. Giordano?"

"Of course," I said. "Thank you for the tea. It was the best I'd ever tasted. Charlie said you import the best."

Meng raised his eyebrows, furrowing his forehead in three wide equidistant arches. "I'm sorry I can't take you to lunch, Genevieve. I have to chopper to JFK. Those Brazilians never keep their freezers cold enough. If I don't inspect, I can lose a lot of money." Meng helped me on with my coat. "I promised Shu Ling I'd take you to dinner with her very soon."

"Oh." My arm caught in my sleeve and Meng let go of the coat so I could shrug it on. "I'm not in New York very much, but maybe next time I come in?"

"I'll tell Shu Ling. She knows all the places you young people like. A couple more things, Genevieve. I didn't mention this to Charlie. Mr. Buhrman called me wondering if I knew anything about Charlie's relationships with women. I said Mr. Greer is happily married, as far as I know, and he should ask Mr. Greer himself. I told him businessmen don't interfere in each other's personal lives."

So, he wanted Charlie to know the Chief suspects him of something. Charlie would be so pissed at the Chief, I wasn't sure I should tell him. He might lose his temper and get himself in trouble. The Chief often tried to rattle Charlie and it usually worked. I pulled on my left glove and extended my right hand to shake good-bye.

Meng touched my fingertips with both of his hands, holding on while he said, "Tell Charlie I thought his article on the snake blood parlor in Taiwan was charming. I told him thank you for letting me read it in rough draft form. If he publishes it anywhere, I'd appreciate it if he removes Meng Produce from mention as sponsor. In fact, Meng Produce doesn't belong in that or any other article he writes."

Meng's abrupt dismissal of public mention of our association told me it was time for me to go. I thanked him again for the tea and left. I heard him pick up the phone and speak in Chinese into it.

As I arrived at the warehouse door, a smiling man handed me a lightweight package. Gold leaf wrapping printed with scarlet Chinese ideograms. I knew it was some of the exquisite tea we'd just shared. Meng was the master of sending mixed messages.

I went out into the chilly morning light, confused and worried. I knew Charlie had sent the article off to a couple of industry trade journals and to some New Age magazine that had offered him three hundred dollars. I hoped he was holding out for more. If not, he'd better get to the editor before Meng wrings his neck and kicks AT out and invites the Canadians in.

I left Meng's office wondering what I was supposed to discuss with "my" Mr. Giordano. Was the fact that Meng knew something about Gianni and me a threat? Who was he threatening? I assumed it was a threat to American Tofu. Maybe to Giordano Brothers. Maybe to me. Did I screw up? I doubted it. The past is the past.

I hurried outside to call Gianni before I picked up Charlie and he started freaking out about Meng and the Canadians. Gianni answered on the first ring. "I don't want this to cause you any problems, Gianni. I'm way over my head. I'm sorry."

He laughed and told me not to worry about anything. "I like it when you're in trouble. It's the only time you call me anymore."

"You told me I should call if I needed to. Friends, remember?"

"Yes, yes. I just enjoy hearing your voice. Forget about Meng. The last time he intimated that he'd give me trouble, he was just crowing. He'd lost a few hundred thousand on some Hong Kong stock. He's using you to play what we call the Chinese cosmetics game," he laughed. "He's saving face, or getting new face. Something. It's not about you or even tofu. Don't worry. I'll take care of it."

***

On the ride home, I drove because I had to tell Charlie about the details of the meeting and I didn't trust him behind the wheel when he blew up. I told him Meng's bad news least to worst: the article, the Canadians, the Chief.

"He doesn't want me to mention his name in the article? Did he say why?"

"No. He doesn't like publicity."

"Yeah, that's his right. It's just Meng Produce, a real modern world business, makes such a great literary contrast to the ancient world of snake blood guzzlers. No problem. I'll fake a name."

"If I were you, I'd run it by Meng."

"I don't go for censorship, Gen. Free speech is just that."

Charlie clung to his principles at the most irrelevant times, like now when he could lock himself into offending his entree into the world's biggest tofu market: Asia.

"Don't think of it that way, Charlie. This article isn't the great American novel. Meng's a precious customer. Show him some deference." He scowled at that. "Give him respect, that's all."

Charlie folded his arms and grumbled, "All right. Not a big deal." Charlie fiddled with the radio while I drove up the interstate, barely keeping up with traffic at eighty. Settling on a classical station, he sat back and said, "Did Meng tell you about the Canadians?"

"Yes. It worries me."

"U.S. Tofu. Can you believe it? The balls to copycat us. Meng and I had a laugh about it."

"You don't think they're trouble? I do."

"Naw. Meng's solid. He wanted to let me know about the competition. That's all. He's watching my back."

Then I turned the questions back to Charlie.

"He said the Chief called, asking about you and your relationship with women."

"What?" Charlie nearly came off his seat so fast he bumped his head on the ceiling. "Ow. That son of a bitch. He asked Nora the same thing. Goddam. I try to do everything I can for him and he goes behind my back to my wife and then to my best customer."

Giordano's your best, I thought. Meng's your favorite.

"I'm gonna have an injunction ordered on him. He can't do this? He's outta control."

"Are you sure? He's probably just doing his job."

"Asking my customers about me and women!" He slammed his palm down on the dashboard. "Implying I'm fucking around! What's Meng gonna think about me and Shu Ling? Pull over. Let me out."

I pulled to the side of the road and he stepped onto the shoulder. He slammed the door and let loose a deep groan that went on and on, sounds a torture victim would make, trying to keep himself from breaking. He stopped and kicked at the shoulder of the road, hollering "Fuck, fuck, fuck, fuck" and kicking the dirt. He lost his balance, regained it, and threw his head back, howling a high-pitched scream.

I'd never seen Charlie lose control of himself like that. I rolled down the window. "You all right?"

He turned around, eyes blazing out from traffic shadows flickering across his face. "What do you think?"

"Charlie?"

"Give me a few minutes. I'll be all right."

I rolled the window up and waited with the car running. When he got back in, he was breathing hard, but quiet.

"She was really a sweet woman, Gen." His voice trembled as if he'd been crying. Leaning back into his hands folded behind his head, he stared out the windshield, oblivious to the stream of oncoming headlights. "She didn't deserve to die. Now the cops are mucking around. Where do they get the right?"

"I don't know, Charlie. Maybe he's following some lead that has nothing to do with you?"

"He doesn't have any leads. He's just on my ass." He sat back, cooled off a little. "You know how a junkie has a monkey on his back? Well, I've got a Burr-man on my back."

I couldn't respond and the joke sank. Then, in a mournful tone, Charlie said, "And I don't know if I can kick it before it sucks me dry."

"Why? Did you do something to him?"

"I don't know. Buhrman doesn't trust anybody. Me? He sees me as the convenient target. He told me he likes to take shooting practice." He'd slipped off his loafers and propped his feet on the dashboard, his eyes examining the murk out the side window. "Maybe when the workers told him Becky liked me, he got a bug up."

"They told him that?"

"They all like me, Gen. That's what Benko said, too. I know it, you know it. I like them, treat everybody right."

What was Charlie telling me? She was a 'sweet woman.' She 'liked him.'

"Charlie, what do you mean, she was a 'sweet woman?'" I waited a long second for him to answer.

"Just what I said. That's all. Nothing else." His voice tailed off so I barely heard him.

"Are you sure you don't want to tell me something?"

"What?"

"Like you knew Becky better than I thought you did?"

The sound of wind grinding past the windows was all the answer I got. We drove the last hour in silence. Charlie turned away from me and stuffing his jacket against the window, he lay his head over and fell asleep.

I knew Charlie as well as I knew any man I wasn't lovers with, probably better because I saw all his weaknesses and didn't make excuses for them,

***

I pulled into my driveway and nudged Charlie. I didn't know if he'd slept or pretended to sleep the last three hours, but I was happy to have the time to myself.

"'Night, Gen. Thanks for driving. Sorry about the tantrum."

"Forget it, Charlie. We gotta talk sometime."

"'Bout what?" he said and slid over into the driver's seat.

I held the door half open, watching him. "You know."

"Sure. Whenever. G'night."

I went inside, read a sweet note from Liam, and listened to my voice mail. Only one message, from Gianni.

"I called Meng. Told him Charlie suggested I call. It's nothing. He just wants me to get him more supermarket business for some of his own products that Giordano distributes for him. I said I'd try. He was just fishing when he guessed that we were involved. Don't worry. Let's talk soon. Ciao, mi amore."

The message sounded like poetry to me. Emotionally whipped, I lay down on the couch. I knew it was weak, an illusion, but I played Gianni's voice over and over, his words kissing, nipping, nuzzling my ears. I lay still a long time, unable to fall asleep.

Visions of Gianni's face close to mine merged into images of him making love to his wife with me standing next to their bed. As I watched them, my hand, my hand more faithful than a husband, more faithful to me than I am to myself, my hand lifted from my stomach and dropped to my lap.

My hand slipped down into my pants. Where Gianni once mounted me, my fingers began to play. Where he sang bawdy songs with his breath, my thumb began to flutter. Where he tickled me with his tongue, my hand began its familiar rhythm. Where he fed on my pomodorini rosa, I opened myself like an empty basket. Where I stretched like a mare to buck him, I tossed myself against his ghost who rose into my mind as real as if I rode him again in the flesh...and then the ghost of my ex-lover Jason rose...and the ghost of my ex-husband Robert...

and vague ghosts of men I've known and men I'll never know, ghosts who always circle me, approaching my hungry skin like servants of my delight when I pleasured myself...and the ghost of Gianni rose groaning into my face again...and the delicious ghost of Gianni whose love I felt lying across me in the bed and then the wet ghost of my own flesh rose into my palm like a wave my whole body felt rushing upwards and back and up and back and when it crashed, I cried out and tears poured out and once again seeing Benko's living ghost, feeling the warmth of his bare chest against mine, my body sagged into my pillows and I drifted off into sleep.

Chapter Five

Charlie

BENKO AND CHARLIE IN THE RING

distracted by lust
I hired the wrong guy
he did his job, I did mine

Rogelio Padilla, my production manager since I started the company, resigned about the time I met Shu Ling. He wanted to move back to Queens where he'd found a job running the night shift at a pudding factory.

We received twenty-five applications for the production manager position.

My first choice was Benko Ivanovich Gladonov, a Russian living in Albany, previously employed as a plant manager at a mincemeat pie factory in England.

I invited Gladonov into my office for a final interview. He'd be number three in the company with tremendous responsibility for every product that went out the door and authority over seventy or so plant employees. I had to make sure he could handle it before I brought him onto the team. I wanted to see how he'd react to a challenge.

"You have everything it takes for this job, Mr. Gladonov. Experience, good references, skill. Only one problem."

"Mr. Greer, yes. My favorite. Problem solving."

"This is not against you, sir. But if I have a hard time understanding you, my Latino and Chinese workers might not get a thing you say."

He laughed, tossing his head back and shaking his long blond hair. "English. Yes. Hard I study. Everything I understand. Ask my old boss. I speak just fine. People? Twenty-two people I boss now in Albany. They know everything I say. Labor? No problem."

"We have seventy in production, a lot more than twenty-two," I said. "Far more complicated. What is your management style? How do you handle people who come late to work?"

"America, Mr. Greer. People come late? One time, I say three strikes and you're out. Three times, bye bye."

Tough love. That sounded reasonable to me. We didn't have a tardiness problem, but he gave a good answer.

"Somebody doesn't show up? The work I take care of it, no matter." He sat across from me as comfortably as any prospective employee I'd interviewed.

Uninvited, he said, "Children, Mr. Greer?"

"Do I have some?"

"Yes."

"Two." I pulled out a snapshot of the kids I'd taken the previous Christmas. Marissa, Little Chuck, and Nora posed beside their presents under our room-sized tree.

"Lovely," he said. "Your wife?"

"Of course."

"Beautiful." Now he smiled at me. "Lucky man."

I smiled and agreed. "I can't legally ask you about your family," I said, leading him to reveal some of his personal information.

"Family? No. I have no children. Wife in England. Ex-wife. New husband and new babies she has. Now happy." He shrugged.

I was glad to hear he had no family because the job required him to be on call twenty-four hours every day of the week. If we needed him, he had to show up. No excuses. I tested him further. "Mr. Gladonov, we need somebody we can count on. Somebody who's not afraid to work."

He interrupted me. "Work, I love. Good working, life tastes sweet. You count on me. So much energy, God gave me. Ask my boss. Two men, three men, I do all that work."

I usually paid no attention to past employer references. Due to employment laws favoring workers, no employer told the truth unless the worker was a real creep, and then they'd barely hint at it, saying "It was better for Mr. X to move on in his career." Still, I'd contacted his employer in Albany and learned that Gladonov had a stellar record. Either his Albany boss wanted to get rid of him, or he wanted to help him. He gave him an unqualified "Great worker" rating. I decided to give Gladonov a chance.

Better be sure, Chuck. You hire him, you're stuck.

"Well, Mr. Gladonov. What do you say we give it a try?"

"Good idea, Mr. Greer. I will give it the old college tryout."

"I'm thinking a three-month probation." I had some doubts about his ability to get along with the workers. On paper, he seemed good enough, but if the factory crew didn't take to him...I'd be right back where I started. "If it works out after that period, we'll hire you with an open-ended contract."

His smile faded and his eyebrows drooped. He gripped his knees with big hands, rocking his body.

"Probation? Like jail? No, I don't take that."

I laughed. "No, not like out of jail. Learning time. You learn about us, we learn about you. We like what we learn, then you're in. It's a critical job, Mr. Gladonov. I have to be careful."

"Yes, I have careful, too. I want green card. I need only less than one year, I have it. Tools, Craftsman I have. Good ones. I work hard all day for you. All night."

Using my tried and true technique of hiring people who need the work the most, I welcomed him to American Tofu with the sense that he could quickly pick up the job from the line supervisors. I could return to dedicating my time and energy to Shu Ling.

I introduced him to the office staff and Genevieve. He charmed us all with his stilted English and his easy smile. I noticed that Genevieve was especially warm to him, volunteering to show him around the plant when he started work. Everyone who met him gave him a cheerful thumbs up. For the first few months as production manager, his smiles and his tools made life in the factory run like an enchanted kitchen in a great castle.

Benko fooled us all and I have only myself to blame, because if I hadn't been so distracted, I could have seen through his "Charming Hardworking Russian Peasant" facade. The way things turned out I don't know if he was the worst or the best hire I ever made. It's no excuse, but I felt so besotted with Shu Ling, I couldn't concentrate on anything else. Her flirting and resistance to my come-ons had built up so much pressure inside me, I wanted any relief wherever I found it.

Having Gladonov in place as production manager turned out to give me the same kind of relief you get when you toss a bone to your neighbor's barking Rotweiler to get it to shut up. If you don't keep tossing it something to gnaw on, it finds its own way to get over the fence and come digging in your yard.

First you shout, then maybe you run, then you hold your ground with a stick in your hand. Then, once the dog makes a move, you do whatever it takes.

Chapter Six

Genevieve

RUSSIAN SAUSAGE

Benko and I had a summer love affair that might have lasted much longer if Becky hadn't died. Although he seemed to enjoy talking to Liam and helping him fix his bicycle, he made it clear that he had no interest in children. That suited me fine. Guys who showed as much interest in my son as in me always ended up proposing, meaning, 'mother me.'

Liam had gone camping in the Adirondacks with his swim team, so I had a luxurious mid-summer week to myself. Feeling a little lonely one afternoon, I invited Benko over that evening to try out a tofu barbecue recipe I'd developed for our seasonal tofu sales. He arrived with a sausage he'd driven two hours round-trip to Buffalo to buy. "Russian aphrodisiac," he said with a big grin.

I complimented him. "Congratulations, Benko. You're learning to flirt."

"Not really," he said. "Flirt I still don't." I showed him the grill and he went to work. "Special spice," he said as he forked the steaming sausage onto my plate.

"No sage, I hope. I'm allergic. It closes up my throat so I can barely breathe."

"No, no. Only special fennel. Opens the heart." He opened his mouth and laughed as he slid a chunk of sausage dripping with grease into his mouth.

"You can flirt, Benko. Don't tell me you can't."

"I learn fast. You like it?"

After a bottle of Chardonnay, Benko and I flopped into my backyard hammock. We swayed in the warm dusk and started kissing. In a few minutes, the mosquitoes drove us inside to a fevered interlude on the couch before we staggered into my bedroom.

Savoring the bubbles of lust that percolated through our veins, we undressed each other slowly, our eyes roaming eagerly across every revelation of the other's body. In the center of Benko's chest, he wore a tattoo of a deep red heart torn into two pieces with blue teardrops cascading down to his belly.

"Don't break my heart again," he said as he watched me examine the tattoo. "Like the others."

I followed the trail of tattoo teardrops down and saw another pink heart-shape peeking out of the elastic of his black briefs. I smiled and he grinned broadly. Benko stayed all night, proving, he said, "the power of the sausage."

"But, Benko," I retorted, "Every cook knows the secret's in the sauce."

His fingers, for all their callused mass, grazed my skin so delicately he felt like my own shadow nuzzling me. He held me gently, following my unspoken instructions perfectly, massaging lonely muscles, tickling sighs from me that I hadn't heard since I lay with Gianni.

That surprising summer night, I snuggled into the cave of Benko's long arms with my head on his chest riding the tranquil rise and fall of his breath into the dreamless night. As the first sun shined through the leaves outside my window, he climbed out of bed to go to the factory.

"Benko, let's keep this between us. Our secret," I said.

"Passion over principle," he replied, groaning tenderly.

"Our secret. Right?"

"Always. Have good dreams. At work I see you."

We saw each other again three nights that week, sleeping together two of them. Benko had enough passion for both of us, aphrodisiac or no. I started calling him 'The Amazing Russian Sausage.'

As far as I knew, Benko and I kept our affair completely quiet. His inbred paranoia coupled with my fear of small-town busybodies spreading gossip forced us to use absolute caution.

When we met at my house, he arrived late, after Liam had gone to bed, and he left before sunrise. The few nights I visited him, I followed the same regimen, showing up late, leaving early, always using his back door. For me, the threat of getting caught added a thrill to our time together.

Benko said he felt at home in our clandestine affair.

"Ferret. I know how ferret lives. Without secrecy, I don't survive," he bragged. "I lived in underground all my life. Anything you want I can teach you how. You get away easy."

I pleased him by pretending to learn every surreptitious and stealthy move from him, and I let him reveal more about himself than he wanted.

Behind his charm and bravado, Benko carried a cold, cynical view of life. He claimed to enjoy our lovemaking more than he had with any other woman, but he never made a sound. He didn't much like to kiss, and when I'd open my eyes from the throes of passion, he'd be staring at me as if he didn't dare let his guard down and surrender to the underworld where feelings rule.

When I asked him what he wanted out of life, more than anything else, he said, "This. What else? I want all I can."

"You must have a dream."

"Yeah. American citizen. Then freedom."

"What then, I mean?"

He closed his eyes and squinted, his cheeks burnished on his high cheekbones.

"Right now, you have ferret eyes," I teased. "Is that what happens when you dream."

"No dream. Thinking about dream." He opened his eyes. "Everybody wants to be movie star in America. Top of the heap, right?" "Not everybody."

"I had chance. One movie. Didn't like it, so I quit."

"You quit?"

"Big money, fame, everybody would know Benko Ivanovich. Gladonov...B-I-G. But nobody would know the real me."

Benko could lie with the best, and he was proud he could, but now I'd caught him. Not that I cared, but he showed what an adolescent mind he had. "What was the film? When?"

"Brit film. Long time ago, over there. Forget the name."

"You must remember the story," I said, egging him on deeper into his fable.

"Stupid story. Oldest story of all. Boy meets girl. Girl sucks boy. Boy fucks girl."

I sat up on the bed. "You were in a porn flick?"

"One time. Not my face. They cut my face off my body. Some smart-ass gay guy, his face on my body in the movie. He never get it up with woman. Dick the size of pinky finger. I quit."

"You mean you acted in the porn and they edited out your face? You're way too cute. Your face is your second best feature."

"Shut up," he snarled, missing my humor. "You're like them. All you want is big cock. I'm not cock. I'm man."

"You're a man, yes you are. I didn't mean anything. It's teasing, that's all." I raised my palm to his cheek and stroked it. "C'mere. Let me kiss your beautiful man's face." I kissed him all over his face and cooed and tickled him until he smiled.

I thought he told the truth about acting in a porn film—he had the equipment—but if he quit, I doubt it was because the editor demeaned him. Benko was the kind of man who, as long as he got paid in money, admiration, attention, he'd perform for more.

I marveled at Benko's physical strength and his stamina. He worked twelve hours in the factory, made love to me for half the night, and awakened refreshed after four hours of sleep.

"Vodka," he said. "Jet fuel. Pure energy. Burns in my veins a pure sun."

My edginess about our affair sent a tiny ripple of peril through my summer. But even without our secret, one other thing kept me really interested in Benko. He had the largest penis I'd ever seen.

It was almost too large for me, and I'm a big woman. He acted so proud of it, especially after the first few times I praised it. About the second week of our affair, I opened my phone and found a text from him.

› check pic ‹

I clicked on the attached image. At first I thought it was a shadowy rose-colored band printed diagonally from one corner of a piece of paper to the other, but when I recognized what it really was, I laughed. He was either showing off or enticing me in his clumsy way, and I didn't totally discount a subtle threat.

That night, I teased him about using Photoshop to magnify the size of his penis. He denied it.

"Prove it," I said.

He unfolded a piece of paper from his shirt, then unzipped his pants. On a regular sheet of printer paper, he'd printed the photo he texted me. He lay his penis against the image on the paper. I burst into laughter.

"Funny?" he snapped. "Funny it's not."

"Oh, Benko, I don't want to hurt your feelings, but it reminds me of a Christmas candle. I can't believe it."

He smiled when I asked him to autograph the paper.

"It's my Christmas candle," he said. "Not always sausage." He signed the photo with a flourish.

"Candles melt," I said, teasing.

"My candle? Never."

I never fully trusted Benko. Someone who boasted about his ability to get away with anything was likely to deceive me, too. In fact, I suspected him of beguiling me already. Yet, that fiery image of his penis exuded a sense of hazard that exhilarated me those summer nights.

If my intuition was right and I ever needed evidence to thwart him, if I ever needed protection from him, perhaps I could use the signed photo so I kept the image on file, at home. If I wanted to continue enjoying the affair, and I did want to, I needed to limit his feeling of power over me that his immense member gave him.

The next time he strutted his erection around my bedroom, dipping and prancing and flapping it like a branch tossing in the wind, I told him he had the thickest one I'd seen, but not the longest.

"No," he said. "Not possible."

"It sure is. Maybe half again as long." I grinned.

"I don't believe you. No one ever told me that."

"You've never been with anyone like me. They're probably just too timid to tell you."

He narrowed his eyes, wilting slightly.

"I'm not saying you've got a pencil there, Benko. Some guys have width, others have length." My knowledge or my experience, or my willingness to compare him negatively, deflated him completely. His puzzled gaze fell on his shrinking limb, rose to my eyes, dropped back. Now I could take charge, swell his cherished limb, and reinflate his confidence. "It's not the size that counts, you know."

"You think I don't know that?" he said defensively. "But most women I slept with don't know that."

"I'm not most women, Benko."

If he was anything, Benko was adaptable. He could change to get something he wanted, so he gave up the boyish bluster about his penis and learned to clown around about it.

"You can be proud of your hands," I said. "Not your cock. You do things with your hands nobody else can."

"From now on," he promised, "my hands I'll use. That's all." "You better have more moves than that," I replied, assuring him that I still appreciated his endowment.

Benko adopted me as his American angel, and I cuddled him as my Siberian bear. A note of mothering crept into my feelings for him and at the same time, a yearning to match his emotional recklessness and free myself from responsibility.

He taste-tested all my new tofu recipes, chuckling and adding vodka to half of them, and he taught me to slake my longing for Gianni. When I let drop that some of the dock men at various produce warehouses had come on to me a little too insistently, he said "You need help, any place, you tell me." With cold eyes and half-snarling, he said, "I take care of them. Nobody knows nothing. Ever."

I shrugged my shoulders.

"It's all right, Genevieve. With me now you're safe."

Chapter Seven

Genevieve

MEAT AND POTATOES

Chief Buhrman asked to see me at home so, naturally, I invited him to lunch. In the middle of November, the day was unbelievably warm—actually it was hot for any day of the year.

I hadn't had time to rake the backyard, so we walked across a crackling brown carpet of oak leaves to the picnic table.

After we commented on the heat and sat down, I explained to Buhrman that he'd entered a wild territory. Once on my property, he had to taste my new tofu recipe.

"I need non-tofu-eating men," I said. "Women like my recipes, but if the husband turns it down, there go half my sales." Charlie had told me to be careful because the Chief was clever and he always went for what he wanted, so I tried to set up a convivial tone for our talk.

"I don't like many new foods," he said politely. "I'm a meat and potatoes kinda guy, like my old man. He lived to ninety-three. I'm not worried about my diet."

He wore a yellow button-down long-sleeved shirt tucked into his khakis. He'd rolled the sleeves up to his elbows in precise folds. New blue running shoes shined on his small white-stockinged feet.

Relieved that he was off-duty, I said, matter-of-factly, "You're in great shape. You must work out."

"It's my policy at the station. All the guys work out," he said as I served him salad. "Something I've kept up since the Marines. Mmm," he murmured, tasting the tofu, "it's okay."

I'd need all my sales and negotiation skills to manage our conversation. I made sure we had plenty of fresh French bread and butter from the farmer's market. His wife had told me he loved iced mint tea so I'd made a jug that morning.

"Do you mind if I take a couple of pictures of you, Aaron? I'm a photographer and I like to shoot people I come into contact with through my job."

"Shoot people?" he said, crossing his hands over his heart in mockery.

"It doesn't hurt. When I develop the photos, I'll give you a copy for Gloria. Maybe for your office."

"I don't mind. Let's take it right now, then we can have our talk?"

"Thanks," I said, and coaxing him to smile and make faces, I took a half dozen shots. It's always amazing how taking someone's picture can loosen them up, if you do it in a spirit of fun. I put my camera back in its case and offered him more tea.

He accepted, saying "Thanks for inviting me over. Can't think of a better thing to do than have a picnic in November. Global warming. It's a good thing." He laughed at his joke. "Not that bad, Jon-a-viv," he said, forking another bite of tofu into his mouth.

He butchered my name as badly as anyone in Clement. "Call me Gen, Aaron. Most people do."

"Gen?" He didn't understand how Gen could be short for Jon-aviv. His hearing was acute, but his processor might have been slow.

"I have to ask you a few questions," he said, swallowing. "You've heard we think the MacDaniel woman was murdered?"

"I hope it's not true. You're the police, Aaron, but it sure looked like an accident."

"Looks are deceiving," he muttered, his eyes glancing away.

"She was a nice woman," I said, not wanting to confront him or his theories even though I doubted she was murdered. Who would benefit from her death? "I didn't really know her, but she was always friendly when I saw her at work."

"Did she have any enemies?"

"I have no idea."

"If you want a lawyer, you can have one," he said, speaking quickly, suddenly serious.

Caught off guard, I hesitated, then I said, "Do I need one, Aaron?" I tried to slow him down by pacing my voice and saying his name, the way I calmed Liam down when he lost his temper.

The Chief went on. "Only you know that. You can have one if you like."

When the Chief first called and asked to meet me, I phoned the Syracuse lawyer. He urged me to keep my conversation with Buhrman neighborly. If the Chief pried into my private life, deny everything, he said. Stay calm. Take notes.

I had a great memory. I wouldn't offend the Chief with taking notes in front of him.

"I'm just wondering how things are going with you and David Golman," Buhrman said.

I should have been ready but my mouth went dry. "We stopped seeing each other quite a while ago." The Chief's tack would be personal. He probably talked to every man I've dated in Clement since I moved here three years ago. Not counting Benko, Golman was the latest. He lasted two months.

"Too bad. He's a good catch. He supports the police and fire retirement fund with a nice donation every year."

"He was always respectful and generous to me."

He nodded, appearing to listen closely, wanting me to say more. "Pretty girl like you. Must be picky, Gloria says. Can't blame you these days, especially with a young boy like yours."

I stiffened. "What do you mean? He's a great kid."

"Oh, I don't mean he's not. Everybody knows he's a good kid. The principal, swim coach, everybody says he's got lots of energy, smart. He's obedient, not like some kids. You trained him real well, Jon-a-viv, I mean, Jon...uh...Gen. I mean, well, finding a man to take on somebody else's son, could be hard. That's all."

"If you were a woman you'd know that's not really a problem, Chief. Most good men prefer mothers." I let my eyes narrow and go cool.

His shoulders rose and he grimaced. "Sorry. No disrespect. Sticking my foot in my mouth again." He softened. "You must drive what, thirty five, forty thousand miles a year?"

"I fly a lot, too. We have customers in every part of the country." Charlie said Buhrman had examined all the AT personnel records. Sounds like he stayed up nights snooping into my expense accounts. Well, let him.

"I was wondering, excuse me for asking, I have to ask, just because, you know, a Chief has to ask the hard questions." He paused while he sipped his tea. He leaned back in the chair and gazed up into the tree. "Bad thing about oaks. Squirrels. I have sycamores in my yard. Squirrels stay away. They don't like the taste of sycamore seeds—stink like rotten fish."

While I waited for him to ask whatever hard question he had, I buttered a thick slab of bread and set it on his plate. He picked it up and nibbled.

Chewing slowly, he asked, "Do you think any of your customers have something against Greer or the company? I mean, any kind of grudges or plans for one of those hostile turnovers?"

"I doubt it," I said, ignoring his obvious Columbo ploy. "No customer would commit a murder to get cheaper tofu. Even if they were crazy. Tofu's not that important in the big scheme of things."

"Now you mention it, there might be a scheme here. I heard that the Chinese guy wants to buy the company. Think he'd put any pressure on Greer?"

"Not that I know of. I don't have anything to do with that side of the business." Buhrman planted a doubt in my mind. Was Charlie really thinking about selling out to Meng? It sounded like one of those buyout rumors that made the rounds of the industry every year or so.

"Charlie's a lively guy," the Chief said.

I nodded, listening.

"Done a lot of good for the town. Made some money. Pretty good reputation with the Chamber and all. You know I talk to pretty much everybody in town?" He leaned forward.

"If I were the Chief, I'd do the same," I said. "You have to know people and let them know you to gain their trust."

Buhrman frowned. "They should trust their Chief no matter what."

The Chief got up and wandered around the yard. I followed. From behind, he looked like a boxer. His wide shoulders and narrow hips and the eager way he leaned forward almost bouncing on his toes belied his laid-back investigator posture.

We meandered to my fall garden. A few stalks of kale and the last Brussels sprouts plants stood green and brave.

I handed him his mug, now filled with fresh ice cubes and tea. I began to wonder why he was really here. So far he'd only confirmed my real distance from the case.

"Ice," he said. "Who'da thought we'd be drinking iced tea, outside, in November?" He shook his head and sipped.

"Got to bring tough things up, Jon-a-viv. Clear everything up, get it out of the way, y'know."

"That's all right, Aaron. I want to help. Ask away."

"Well...did you ever hear anything about Charlie and the dead woman?

"No. Nobody's said anything." So, Charlie and Becky must have been fooling around and the Chief's sniffed it out. I'm glad I didn't ask him the other night in the car. I'm a lousy liar, and Buhrman would pick it up right away. Using an old sales trick, I reversed the focus. "Have you?"

"There's something in the wind, but no, not directly. I know he and his wife have been getting counseling for quite a while..."

"They've been under a lot of strain since the death, even before. Trying to build a unique business like this, from nothing, it's worse than a roller coaster. Charlie says he feels like he's always at war." We stood beside each other contemplating the yard.

Eventually, Buhrman said, to the side of my face, "You know him pretty well, don't you?"

"Pretty well. After him and Nora, you could say I was next in line. I love the company. He gave me a great job when I needed it and nobody else came through."

He shot a skeptic's narrow eye at me. "But if it came down to the truth or your friendship? Or your job?"

He knew I'd say "The truth, of course," and I did. I added, "It's the right way to go, isn't it." He nodded, and I said, "Safest, too."

He turned and smiled. "Truth. That's my motto. One little word. If only everybody believed in it. We'd have world peace, health, happiness, it would be heaven on earth."

He was such a dissembler—no doubt it takes a liar to catch a liar.

"Is there something you want to tell me about Charlie, Aaron?" "No, no." He avoided my eyes. "Just checking on the scuttlebutt about him and MacDaniel. Lotsa rumors flying around town."

"I haven't heard that one." Or even suspected it until the other night on the drive home from Meng's. I kept walking, pointing out my wilted white Peace roses, planning my answer. "Those roses are one of the best things about my house. They were beautiful right up to the frost we had last week."

Buhrman touched a blossom. Every petal fell, drifting to the ground, white leaves speckled with brown rot.

"Lotta nice gardens in Clement. Great town for gardens." When he straightened up he said, "I hear it's real nice down in the Berkshires this time of year..."

Maintaining my slow breathing, affecting indifferent tone, I said, "I love it over there. The hills are too flat for Alpine but cross-country skiing in the winter is wonderful. Or used to be."

He wrinkled his eyebrows and pursed his lips, obviously expecting me to tell him more, so I continued. "In the summer, sometimes I go to Tanglewood to hear classical music. Liam and I go every summer, since he was four. We sit on the lawn, light a candle, listen to live music. Total peace. Do you ever go there?"

"Naw. We like country music."

Then he swallowed a long drink of tea and I continued. "I have friends who live near there but I haven't visited them for quite awhile."

We'd ambled around the yard and ended up back at the picnic table. The Chief set his glass on a napkin and frowned. "Would that be the Jewdanos?"

Buhrman mispronounced the name without a hint of irony. "You mean the Giordanos." I laughed. "Yes. Giordano Brothers is my customer in New York."

"What kind of relationship would you say you have with Mr. Jewdono?

"What do you mean, Aaron?"

"Personal or professional?"

"Professional and personal. We're friends. I'm friends with all my customers. It's the key to my success."

He stuck out his lower lip and scratched his temple. "You know, I heard about this big competition you had with Greer, see who could sell the most tofu?"

"Yeah, a little game we played to keep things interesting"

"You won, right?"

"Yeah. What does that have to do with anything?"

"You win any prize or anything?"

He knew what I won and I felt so defensive I wanted to pick up the tea pitcher and pour it on his head. I was long done with Gianni and he had no right...but I had to play it cool.

"A trip to Cancun. Not only that, Charlie had to wash my car inside and out ten times."

"Jewdino give you the winning edge, did he?"

"You could say that. His sales grew fastest."

He stopped and breathed, letting his shoulders sag. Peering into his teacup and speaking as if he'd memorized a script, he said, "Can you explain to me if a personal relationship with a customer that brings you personal reward is not a breach of ethics?"

"What are you talking about? If you're in sales, you don't want customers, you want friends."

The Chief flabbergasted me. I had to deflect his aggression again. "Aaron, are you insulting me or accusing me of something?"

"Sorry, Jon-a. Just asking things. Need your help to figure out motives and such."

"What motives?"

He raised his brows and smiled without opening his lips.

I spoke in a soft, sisterly voice, as helpful as I could be. "Aaron, I'm afraid you're naive about business. Ever been in business?"

Clarity came into his eyes. "No, law enforcement was my calling, since I was ten years old."

"In business, it's not all tooth and claw. People help each other all the time. That's how it's done."

"They help each other break the law. Big companies, little companies...they help each other all right."

Exasperated, I continued, wanting to lecture him. "Anything I did with Giordano or any other customers that you might construe as personal, we always followed the bonds of propriety."

He nodded in agreement. "I believe you. Don't blame you for being upset with me, but it's my job to sniff around. Gotta stir things up to see what happens."

I laughed, trying to lighten up. "Like flour when you make bread. Stirring the flour so it rises evenly."

"I guess. Gloria takes care of our baking and cooking. I take her over to White Owl's, Wegmans or such, she and I shop together. She points, I pick up what she says.

"No doubt she's a great chef."

"The best."

We'd circled back to the garden. "Best smelling flower in the world, rose," he said. "I should come back in the summer to smell them."

"Please," I said, "come by any time. Some of these roses get as big as cantaloupes. You can smell them from the deck."

"Interesting," he said, distracted. He turned toward me, looking past, toward the house. "So anyway, Jordina. I'm going to visit him. Go down to Hunts Point and get a feel."

"When? Why?"

"No stone unturned," he said. "I told Greer I was sorry I had to interrupt with your customers, but, you never know."

"I better call him to let him know, Aaron. If you just show up, Giordano could get the wrong idea."

The Chief picked up his mug and sipped at the iced tea. "Sure, give him a call." He set the mug down. "Y'know, Jon, 'scuse me, Gen...life in Clement's real nice. Outta the way. Good place to raise kids..."

"Yes, Liam likes it here. The school's much better than his last one."

"My wife said she felt sorry for you."

"Why?"

"Said it must get lonely for a single woman, young professional woman like you. Good-looking."

"Thank you." I smiled as modestly as I could, trying to gain some control in the conversation. Politeness and form went a long way with the Chief. "Sometimes it's lonely. I'm not that interested in getting involved right now. Between my son and my work, who has the time or energy?"

"I don't mean to be invading, here, but you understand. It's complicated, this murder thing. Was it a murder? Here I can only go with my gut. If somebody gets away with it, everybody in town's in danger. Right?"

"I pray to God it's nothing like that."

"Me, too."

"Well, I gotta ask a few difficult questions. You're doing fine, like Gloria said you would."

I wondered if he thought what he'd already asked and implied was easy. "Shall we sit down, Aaron?"

"No, no. I talk better if I keep moving. Walking or driving. Don't have the cruiser or we could take a ride. Anyways, you have a nice yard."

I was sure Buhrman didn't consider me involved in the "murder," until his next question.

"Now what about this Benkowander Popov or Smirkov or whatever?"

"Gladonov."

"Gladenuff. Strange name. Guess he's a happy guy?" He barked a tiny laugh. "He's your friend, right?"

"Yes. I'm friends with the people I work with."

"I thought you weren't friends with the dead woman. She's worked there at least a year."

Flustered, I said, "Aaron, you're making me feel like you're accusing me of something and I don't know what."

"No, no. It's friendly. I just never did one of these murder investigations before. I had training a long time ago, but, you know." "Okay. No problem, long as you're not involving me."

Not answering directly, he went on. "We're not sure about this case, you know, but we gotta go on with the investigation: double murder, you know. Last thing—by the way, that salad wasn't bad—this Gladnuff comes over here sometimes?"

"Sure. I invite different people over from work. To try out recipes. Charlie likes me to. Says it promotes the team spirit. I'm a good team player."

He muttered, "I bet you are."

When he said that, I realized nothing I said would make him trust me. He fired his next question at me like a trial lawyer.

"Do you know where Gladenuff was the night of the murder?"

I ignored this continual reference to "murder." I hoped Buhrman was only a backcountry cop who identified with the prosecuting attorney on the TV courtroom shows and learned his interviewing techniques from them, but with every question, I doubted that more and more. "All I know is he said he was at the woman's birthday party."

"Yeah. Him and those other rowdies you've got working for you. Wild party, they say. If Gladkop lets anything slip, about the woman, anything, I'd appreciate it if you let me know right away. There's scuttlebutt around that he knew the dead woman, in the Biblical sense. He denies it. But I can't help wonder if that was a little Russky she had inside her when she died." He stood up. "Would sure make it easy if we had some way of telling."

"What about DNA testing?" I asked. "Seems like it's the latest thing."

"We're working on it. Takes time, is all. First the machines screwed up. New operators, they said. Probably some Chinaman just off the boat. Now they tell me it'll take a little while to match the samples with the results."

"Must really frustrate you, Aaron."

"Yeah, well, I'm used to it, small town, upstate and all. Good thing is, D.A.'s not worried. He's with me all the way. Jona... Gena...I'll get the DNA."

I smiled. "Does it really matter, Aaron?"

He stared at me, his mouth open, as if he couldn't believe such a foolish question. "It could be the key to the whole investigation."

"Oh." My smile disappeared. "Guess I don't understand these complicated investigations. Selling tofu is about as complicated as I can get," I said, playing his game.

"Well, don't worry about it. He forced a grin up at me with tight thin lips. "Thanks for lunch, Jona. Gloria must've told you about the tea? It was good."

"No sugar added, Aaron. Just good old New York clover honey. Straight from the farm."

"Everything lived up to your reputation, like Gloria said it would.

"I'll send her some of my recipes."

"No, you don't have to do that."

"No, really, I'll send them from the office."

"Maybe she'll change 'em, fix 'em up a bit for me." The Chief laughed, I laughed. "If anybody can make me eat that stuff, it's her," he said. "No offense."

He smoothed his thick black hair and said, "I know it's tough being a newcomer here. You've been here what? A few years? Gloria and I have lived here twelve years already. We still feel like the natives' favorite TV show."

"I've felt that, too."

"Yeah, you'd be surprised what people know about you," he said. "Well, thanks again. If you think of anything, let me hear from you."

"Good luck, Aaron. I'm sure you'll figure everything out before long."

He opened his car door and turned back. "Watch out for stray bullets," he said.

Taken aback, I said, "What?"

"The war, you know. Greer's tofu war."

I glared at him. "You scared me, Aaron. Don't do that."

He sputtered, "I'm sorry. Just trying to joke."

I paused and made what I hoped was a schoolmarm's face, admonishing him. He dropped his eyes.

"It's okay," I said. "I always think of Clement as safe—no guns, no bullets."

He stared away from me, nodding, then climbed into his car and rolled down the window. "I'm paid to keep it that way."

"Say hello to Gloria," I said, and waved good bye. As soon his tail lights disappeared, I went inside and made myself a cup of black tea and sat down to think.

***

The Chief had targeted every man in my recent life. Golman and the other men in town could handle themselves.

I didn't worry about Gianni. If he had to, he could prevent Buhrman from getting too close.

If the rumor about Charlie and Becky was true, Charlie could be in big trouble. Not for having the affair—that would color his reputation and who knows what Nora would do—but for denying it to the Chief.

Ten minutes after Buhrman left, I packed a bowl of tofu salad and got in my car to drive to Benko's. For all the reasons he'd fretted about, it seemed he'd end up bearing the brunt of Buhrman's scrutiny. He was foreign, he knew the woman, maybe too well. I'd have to ask Benko about his 'Biblical knowledge' of Becky.

As with the rumor of Charlie and Becky, I suspected the Chief was spreading hearsay, hoping to frighten Benko. Buhrman's suspicion about the 'little Russsky' worried me but I didn't see how it was possible that Benko had been sleeping with Becky. I'd kept him busy most of the summer.

Right then Benko needed me to coach him in his dealings with Buhrman. If he reacted the same way that got him in trouble in Russia, or the way he'd promised me he would if he received the least threat from the Clement police, Buhrman would have him in jail in five minutes. He may not be deported, but he'd be back on the road in America with millions of other aimless immigrants.

I wanted to help him but, as I drove across town, the Chief's warning reverberated. "...you'd be surprised what people know..."

I had to be realistic. I couldn't take any sides here, except mine and Liam's. I drove by Benko's, turned my car around, and headed home. No matter how much I tried, I couldn't help Benko and he'd take on Buhrman as a personal challenge, anyway, no matter what I said. Benko would need all his survival skills and cleverness.

Now I had to to shelter myself from any trace of suspicion in Buhrman's mind. I had to distance myself from Benko and keep it that way as long as the investigation lasted. Chief Buhrman had just packed my sizzling summer affair with the 'Amazing Russian Sausage' deep under ice.

Chapter Eight

Genevieve

CHARLIE'S PECCADILLO

Charlie called at 11:00 p.m. the night before our quarterly sales trip to Philadelphia.

"Will you drive, Gen? My back's acting up."

The next morning, I rushed out of the house to pick him up by six. A big grin rolled across his face when he opened the door of my Volvo wagon. He'd spotted my running gear on the passenger seat.

"What's this?" he said, dangling a pair of my underpants between his fingers. "Ready for any emergency?" He scooped up my pants and shorts and bra and shirt and running shoes stuffed with soggy socks and tossed them into the back seat.

"You know me, Charlie—I gotta move. Since you've made me spend so much time in my car, I'm always ready to run. Sometimes I spot a lovely woods and I have to explore it."

I knew I didn't have any choice about the road trips. When Liam and I decided to settle in the country, I accepted the fact that

I might have to travel to make a living. Fortunately Liam liked staying with Carla whenever I was out of town. She let him play computer games until well after his bedtime, but I didn't really mind.

Charlie would do just about anything to keep me on the road, so it was easy to get him to pay her a stipend if I stayed away over night. When I drive alone on the highway, I never listen to the radio or CD's because my mind keeps me company.

But if I ride with someone, especially Charlie, I love to talk and tell him stories of my life. He believed I was the wildest, freest woman he'd ever heard of. Sometimes I wonder if he didn't ask me to go on trips with him just so he could listen to the adventures of my youth. This trip was different. He had to talk.

"I don't want to sound too personal? But have you had a lot of lovers?"

"Enough. Why?"

"I haven't had many. Really just Nora. I don't count the five before her as real lovers. They were more like warm-ups."

"Sounds like you have plenty of experience, Charlie." I didn't want him to feel lacking in the manhood department.

"Nora knows about them," he said. "We talk about everything. Well, almost. Some stuff, you talk about it? It takes on a life of its own nobody needs."

"What do you mean?"

"I'm tempted sometimes by other women," he admitted, "but not enough to take action. The kids are young and I wouldn't want to throw a monkey wrench into our marriage."

I kept my expression flat, incurious.

"Sometimes it's miserable. Nora's gone a lot now, golfing afternoons, taking classes at night. She's hanging out at the country club. We don't sleep together, you know what I mean, very often. When we do, though, it's still great. I guess that's what's most important. I mean, with the murder—the death, I mean—all the heat I'm taking."

Charlie rolled his window down and stretched his arm out, playing with the wind, swooping and slicing his open palm around, like a little boy. "It's a good thing we go to therapy every week. We work out most of our problems there. You know, I know you have a hard life, Gen, single mom'n all. Being married's just as tough. Still, I wouldn't give it up."

Since Nora and I had started running together, we'd gotten to know each other better. We found we could work out some of the stress the death had infected our lives with by slow jogging while we talked.

No wonder she spent so much time away from home and Charlie. When they were together, he probably moaned and groaned non-stop. She was reserved and the pressure of the investigation had started to show on her, but she opened up a little more with every run.

I didn't respond to Charlie's invitation to discuss his marriage, a subject I already knew too much about. We rode in silence most of the first hour, both of us half-asleep.

***

I'd been up late on the phone the night before, listening to Benko complain about work, about his horniness, about my cruelty for not letting him come over.

"You dump me, Genevieve. I don't like that. Not the kind woman you used to be. Not like Russian girls, all beautiful and mean. Sweet Genevieve. Sweet creamy Irish lassie." He laughed, then his voice turned sinister. "You leave me? Big trouble you never know."

I'd talked with him three or four times a week by phone since I stopped seeing him, mainly to keep track of him and to keep him on the far end of a string, a string I kept taut and tried to lengthen with every phone call, one that he tugged and tried to reel around his finger with his gruff charm.

The night I told him that we had to stop seeing each other because of the Chief's suspicions, he'd barged into my house, charging up my front stairs red-faced and growling. He refused to believe me about Buhrman's snooping.

I tried to gentle him with hugs and soft words. When I wouldn't kiss him, he threw me down on the couch and ripped at my shorts. I yelped, not loud enough to wake Liam, but sharp enough to surprise Benko.

Claiming innocence, he blustered, "Before, you like rough." "Benko, get out of here right now."

He shoved me down again. "Don't play hard to get."

I pulled myself up and slid off the couch and ran to the phone. "If you don't leave right now, I'll call the police. You'll never see citizenship."

He got hold of himself, barely. Trembling and panting, he stormed around the room. "You be sorry. You're like every other woman. My big cock you want. You gotta have it."

"I want more from a man than his cock. I don't care how big it is." I was as angry as he was.

He ignored me. "You'll never see it again. Till you beg. For my sausage, you'll beg. I'll laugh." He turned and left, rattling the windows as he slammed the door. I locked it behind him and sagged to the floor, weak in every muscle. I slouched against the door for a long time, letting my heart settle down.

The phone rang. It was Benko. "I'm sorry, Gennee. You beautiful woman. I make you feel good. Not bad like I did."

"Benko, you scare me."

"I'll be good, don't worry. Fun we can still have. In more secret now. No Chief can catch me."

"I can't see you, Benko, somebody might see us. If the Chief finds out, we're both in big trouble. Besides, you scared me just now—you don't control your temper. If I say I don't want you to come over, you have to listen to me."

"Oh, Gennee, whatever you say."

"We can talk on the phone. Let's see how you behave."

"Honey. I know we'll be so close. Best woman I ever had. We have best phone sex you ever tried."

"We'll see, but I don't think I could handle that with you just a mile away."

"See what I mean? You want me."

"Good night, Benko."

"Tomorrow yes? Phone date?"

He hung up. Maybe I'd have to talk with Benko on the phone every night to keep him under control, but phone sex? I'd have to be so horny and lonely I couldn't resist. Then we may as well have the real thing.

***

I came out of my fugue as the car followed its nose toward the New Jersey Turnpike. We stopped for lattes at a rest area, and while we waited for service, Charlie launched into one of his obligatory management conversations. Every month he gave his managers a one-on-one pep talk based on *Harvard Business Review* or *Fast Company*'s lead article. That month it was self-forgiveness as the basis for top performance.

We got back into the car and he changed the subject to one of his favorite topics: the difference between men and women. As usual, I had to let him ramble on for a while until he wormed his way around to what he really intended to say. "You know, Genevieve, I could never be a woman. I'm not brave enough to go through birth," he began.

"Charlie, where've you been? You can be a woman and not have a baby."

"Would that be a complete woman?" he answered, challenging me. "If you can't fulfill your biological destiny, wouldn't you feel frustrated? Be maybe a little less than you can be, totally?"

"I disagree. Who says biological destiny is the most important destiny? Who says a baby is a woman's biological destiny, just because she can?"

Charlie stuck out his chin at the windshield. "If you don't give a hundred per cent of yourself, you'll never be your real self."

I waited. Charlie was wound up about something.

"Your real self is a moving target. In Zen, they say it's your original face. The one you were born with. I always wonder how that can be, especially after you grow a beard, or get wrinkles." He chuckled. "I see my baby pictures and say where'd I lose my original face? Maybe when I got married. Maybe it's the business. Maybe the time's coming for me to try out a monastery for a while. Let all this commotion go. Simplify. How do you keep your life simple?"

"I don't even try and don't think a woman has to have a baby to be her full self. You're really out of touch if you think that."

"Don't get mad. I'm a feminist."

"Sure you are. But for me what's true is, my raising Liam by myself is what gives me strength."

"I can see that. You face death square in the face when you give birth, you survive. You can handle anything after that. That's what I mean." Charlie grinned. "Bold. It's what you get when you go all out. Risk everything. You don't have a choice, so you give it everything you've got. Like being an entrepreneur."

I sensed Charlie tugging himself back on track to pump himself up with the self-esteem speech. He needed to listen to himself to find his own courage in the middle of the company's troubles.

"Genevieve, we have to have a serious talk for a minute."
"What have we been doing, Charlie?"

"About business, I mean. Meng and Giordano. What shall we do? You haven't told me what you think yet. It might be a bigger problem than we thought. I know you and Giordano are through, but I fucked up, too. Somebody outside my marriage. It's a little thing. You know what a peccadillo is?"

"It's a sex toy, Charlie. Everybody knows that."

"Don't mock me. It's a little sin, is all. Everybody does them. Maybe mine's worse than your affair with Giordano. I'm married." I kept my eyes on the road.

Charlie sighed and said, "I've been fooling around with Shu Ling Meng since last summer."

I slammed the steering wheel. "My god, how could you?" I had a feeling about that when he and Shu Ling came back from a 'meeting' and Charlie's face stayed flushed all afternoon.

"I'm afraid Buhrman's gonna find out and then the whole town will know. Right now he suspects that Chinese worker did the deed. He'll assume that I'm in on it. Then, 'That's all she wrote, Charlie.' I'm destroyed. Maybe it was the Chinese guy, but I had nothing to do with it." His voice pleaded.

"I know you didn't. Everybody knows you didn't. Stop saying you didn't. You're calling attention to yourself."

"What should I do?"

"Does Nora know?"

"No. Thank god."

"Does Meng? "

"I'm afraid he might. Maybe not. I hope not. I'm not gonna ask." "He'll keep quiet. He doesn't want his family involved. Make sure Shu Ling doesn't admit anything."

"She won't. She's a tough little empress."

"Empress? You're nuts, Charlie. Does she have kids?" I waited for Charlie to answer but he had rolled down the window and started playing with the wind again.

In a quiet voice nearly obliterated by the sound of traffic, he whined, "No. She doesn't want children."

Thank god, I thought. The last thing he needed was to get seriously involved with this spoiled witch. I grabbed his arm and squeezed it hard. "What about your kids? What about Nora?"

He shrugged his shoulders.

"Don't be stupid, Charlie." I squeezed again and he pulled away. "You have to stop with her right now." I was nearly screaming. "You said it. Stop and deny you ever had anything to do with her. Call her right now." Catching him while he was vulnerable and open, I handed Charlie my cell phone. "Hurry up. If you want to save your family and the rest of us, call her."

"Why? We messed around but we never slept together."

"Christ, Charlie. Wake up. Did you hear yourself a minute ago? It doesn't matter if you slept together or not. If the word gets out you were playing around with her, we're all screwed. I don't care what you do for yourself. Think of the rest of us for once."

"It's innocent. All about communication, not sex. Like the bonobos, those little monkeys? They never fight. Just caress each other, make love. If any one of them gets mad or hurt, they just fuck all their conflicts away."

"That's what you want to be, a bonobo?"

"No, of course not. But they're in our genes. They use sex to keep things in harmony. I call them the original 'Make-Love-notWarriors.'"

Impatient, I said "Did you ever hear about evolution? We're not apes. They're in your genes, not mine."

"In my jeans like my pants?" Charlie laughed hard, nearly choking. "Lighten up, Gen. Sometimes animals know more than humans. It's a game. I'm learning about communicating with women. Shu Ling's an expert."

I was as stubborn as Charlie was deceptive. I began to lose my temper. "Shu Ling's a little slut. She's got a hook in your dick and she's dragging you around by a line of bullshit." His self-justifying narcissism pissed me off as much as my ex-husband's.

"Why are you so upset, Gen? It's nothing."

"If you're a bonobo, Mr. Meng's the big gorilla and he'll bash your head. You're blowing it, Charlie. Remember, it's not just you involved here."

He groaned. "This is what I get for following my dreams."

"Stuff the self-pity and stop whining. Make the call or I will." I stared at him with all the fury and disgust I could shoot out of my eyes. Make Love Not Warriors?

He lifted the phone to his ear and then let it drop into his lap without dialing. "Do I have to do this?"

I screamed at him. "Do it and shut the fuck up." I'd never lost my temper with him before, but between his gullibility and Benko's bullying, all my patience was squeezed dry.

He dialed Shu Ling's number and listened for a long time and then left a message.

"Thank you, Charlie," I said, relieved that he'd taken the first step, but I had to keep pressure on him, or he'd backslide. "Keep trying. After our appointment, you take the car into New York to talk to her. I'll take a bus home."

"Jesus, Gen. A bus'll take all night. Fly."

At least he'd agreed to go to New York but, to break up with her? Or was this a good excuse for him to get laid? Maybe

I should back off and tell Nora and let her work it out with her husband.

"The company can afford it. Fly."

Charlie's compliance turned the tables on me, as if he were calling my bluff. I meant what I said and if he didn't break up with her, I was ready to make a change anyway. Tired of Benko, exhausted from keeping the business together, I was fed up with the Chief's antagonism.

"All right, I'll fly. But if you don't break up with Shu Ling right now in your mind and, and..." He nodded his head in time to a song playing on the radio, as if he were alone. "Charlie. Listen to me. You break up with her today, or you and I are done. I mean it."

He glanced at me then back at the highway. "I get it. It's important. But the movie..."

"The movie means shit to a dead company. Christ, Charlie. Where's your brain?"

He grinned, nodding and glancing down at his lap.

"Don't mess around with me. This is life and death serious," I said. Charlie was incorrigible. He thought he could charm his way out of anything.

"What's the difference between me and Shu Ling and you and Giordano? C'mon. I mean it."

He didn't need to know anything more about Gianni and me. "The obvious thing is Gianni and I ended it a long time ago. He cared about me. Shu Ling's using you. She doesn't care about you."

"Yes, she does."

"I mean it, Charlie. Don't bullshit me. I'll quit and tell Nora why."

"God, don't let the mice abandon ship," he mumbled.

"Shut up. I'm not going anywhere. I have to support my kid. Stop feeling sorry for yourself."

He sat staring out the window into the harvested fields. "I guess you're right. I feel relieved I told you about us," he said. Abruptly he turned to me. "Gen, if this works out and you get that cookbook done, you can have a twenty percent royalty on every copy we sell. Liam's college education will be all set."

"Just straighten out your fucking life, then tell me how much money I'll make."

Charlie told the truth—his brains hung down below his belly button. The only logic he understood was the yang of his balls and the yin of the Chinese girl's crotch. All Meng needed to transfer his business to the Canadians was a simple implication about Charlie's ethics. Worse, that would ruin us in the marketplace. Charlie knew it, he sweated it, but he kept seeing that woman.

"I'll go with you, Charlie. I promise I'll sit quietly and when it's done, I'll take you out for Thai food and a bottle of wine. We'll stay in the city and you can cry on my shoulder all night. I won't tell a soul in Clement."

"Give me a break, Gen. It's not that bad. Anyway, I need to do this with class, in private. Her and me. I know I have to let her go, but I want to stay friends. Her film might be worth millions in sales over the next few years."

I wasn't sure he would follow through, but I agreed to let him handle it, mostly because I couldn't stand to be with him that day any longer than I had to.

When we got to Philadelphia, Charlie couldn't focus on the sales meeting. He kept checking his watch, fumbling with his cell phone, generally ignoring what our distributor had to say. So I ran the meeting and we left with a commitment for business in a hundred new stores. Charlie was so distracted he didn't even comment or thank me.

On the way out to the airport, I broached the other taboo subject. "All right, Charlie. Truth or consequences. We have to clear up one more thing."

"What's truth?" he asked.

"Don't play games."

"I'm not."

"All right. The *truth*," he said, stiffening and gripping the steering wheel. "You can trust me. You know that. Better than anybody else. Maybe even yourself." He smiled but faced away.

The traffic was heavy and sometimes Charlie spaced out when he was driving. I asked "Shall we pull over? You make me nervous sometimes."

"I got a long trip ahead of me. Let's get you to the airport and I'll paddle on upriver to the Big Island."

"You sure you can talk and drive?" He'd always been an inconsistent driver, missing stop signs, weaving in and out of traffic, getting lost. Now he was deeply upset.

"Sure. Let's talk. We can talk anything now, Gen. We pretty much hit bottom."

"Maybe you hit bottom. I call it being smart. If you don't give up Shu Ling, you'll hit the real bottom."

"I know. I play it stupid sometimes." He grinned, trying to charm me into absolving him for his idiocy. "Thank god for my luck. And for you and Benko and Nora. Without you guys, I'd probably be in a nuthouse right now."

"We'll make it, Charlie. We're in this together."

"I'm countin' on it. Countin' on you. Sorry, Gen, but you're the best. Don't groan. It's true. That's truth."

"Don't flatter me, Charlie."

"Shut up, Gen. You said truth. That's it."

I spoke quickly in a matter of fact tone to keep him talking. "This is it: you and Becky. What happened?"

"Oh, shit," he said, rolling his eyes back and smirking. "I knew it. I've known it for months."

"The Chief says there's a rumor around town about you and her. Don't you see that's as bad as you and Shu Ling?"

"Sure I do. If it was true, it's worse. But you know who's spreading that rumor?"

"Who?"

"Our good old public servant, Aaron Buhrman."

"Why in God's name would he do that? He's an honest cop."

"Ambitious cop. He's trying to make up something to build his career on. He came up with that 'rumor' on the spot in my office after Becky died. Now he's using her to claw his way out of Clement to Albany, or some other ginned-up police station job."

Charlie might have Buhrman pegged, but he was too defensive. I wanted the full story about him and Becky. "The Chief's been straightforward with me and very polite and considerate with everybody in the company."

Charlie's teeth ground, sending ripples from his jaw up across his temples. "Here's how it is. First, he fucked with me. Then he fucked with all our workers, asking them about me and women, especially Becky. Can you believe that? Then he interferes with Meng, and Giordano. Now he's threatening you. Goddam slimy blight on society out to crush me on his way up!"

He was tailgating the car in front of us at seventy miles an hour. I shouted at him "Slow down. You're gonna kill us."

He slammed on the brakes and backed off from the car ahead and said, "Sorry."

"All right," I said.

"Don't mean to take my frustration out on you."

"Don't worry."

"Buhrman's on my ass and I don't know what to do."

"Stay cool, Charlie. He's trying to do his job and if he's a little dim and has to resort to rumors...don't take him so seriously. I don't."

"You don't?"

"It's gonna blow over. Relax. Let him do his cop thing and stay on course. Be smart."

"I'm trying." Charlie pulled over at the Continental Airlines terminal.

"Good luck in New York, boss," I said. "I'm with you. Don't think about the rumors. Nobody believes them."

"They better not," he said. "I'm gonna do this and I'd appreciate it if you let me tell Nora—when the time comes."

Always negotiating, Charlie stared at me as if we were ironing out the last details of a business contract. I nodded and said, "I don't want to mess up your marriage, Charlie. You do that on your own."

"Thanks," he said and pulled away, waving, a grim expression replacing his usual smile.

While buying my ticket for the next flight home, I realized that Charlie didn't answer my question about him and Becky. Either he respected me enough not to lie to me, or he feared me enough to evade telling the truth.

I called Giordano Brothers from the air to set up an appointment with Gianni. He'd mentioned a couple of jobs last year. They'd sounded good but at that time, they were too far away. Now, I had to be ready to get out of American Tofu. Either Charlie the bonobo or Benko the sausage is likely to wreck everything.

Chapter Nine

Charlie

IMPORTS FROM CHINA

gosling kicks, webbed feet
splash free, cold wind calls
strong wings storm empty blue sky

Driving north from Philly, I called Shu Ling and left a message asking her to meet me at the Empire Hotel, on Broadway across from Lincoln Center. I wanted to go down to Shu Ling's apartment but it relieved me when she insisted on coming uptown to my hotel.

I was afraid I'd lose my sense of purpose if I had the chance to sink into Shu Ling's black leather couch and sniff the perfumes of the exotic flowers that turned her apartment into a jungle. Her bedroom at my back would tantalize my mind with Simian Soles or some other tempting monkey love "practice" Shu Ling teased me with.

My other voice chimed in with Genevieve's hissing at me to break up with Shu Ling.

Forget Shu Ling. Calm Genevieve down. If she leaves you, bye bye American Tofu.

Jiminy's right, as usual. If Genevieve left while we're vulnerable from the investigation, we might lose Giordano. Since Giordano made way too much money from our products, he wouldn't fly the coop overnight. But I didn't need the uncertainty her leaving would cause.

Yet, behind her threat and the angst it would give me, I sensed that she might be the most crucial person to have on my side throughout the whole fiasco.

No matter what I did with Shu Ling, I faced an immense sacrifice. To save American Tofu, for my family, for eighty-three workers and their families, Genevieve insisted I had to give up the potential of the most amazing love affair I could imagine. I had to be a hero, but nobody could know but me and Genevieve, and it wasn't heroics to her.

I never thought of myself as any kind of Super Hero. I'd rather have a love affair with Shu Ling than leap tall buildings. Except for the investigation, tofu was getting boring and a life with Shu Ling would be wild and exciting.

Chuck, Chuck, listen to yourself. You don't know Shu Ling at all. Shu Ling's using you. Cruising you. Abusing you.

Yeah, I've been using her, too. So what?

She's too hot. She's the flame you can never tame. You'll have no money, no family, no fun, no fame.

I know. I know. Sometimes you have to take the heat.

Charlie Greer, fire fighter. You think you can piss on the fire and put it out? You got so much heat on you right now, it's singed your brain. Watch your life flow down the drain.

Even if I was willing to give up everything for Shu Ling, Could I survive in her world? Adventure, excitement, transformation into a wild Taoist lover? Am I thinking too short-term by sticking with the company no matter what happens? I don't have to worry about losing everything because I barely have any net worth anyway. Lots of people would want to hire me. Or I could start another business whenever I want. Nora? She would protect herself, but what about the kids?

I didn't worry about the kids. They were the most beautiful beings in my life. Chuckie made me laugh with his constant clowning around and his drive for soccer. He knew how to break out of the pack and score, sort of like his old man. Rissi... so precious, soft, snuggly. She already played the piano like a ten-year-old and she was in first grade. She could play ragtime and Chopin well enough to make me cry. I'd stay in their lives no matter what. I loved them more than I loved anybody else, yeah, I hated to say it but it was true. I loved them more than I loved their mom, so whatever happened, I'd be there for them.

Driving toward the city that afternoon, my mind spun out of control. At one point, as I sped up sulfurous New Jersey Turnpike toward the Holland tunnel, I made up my mind to blow off everything. I'd sell the business to Meng for the best price I could get and sign on as Shu Ling's manager. Then I'd build her movie career into a spectacular success and she and I would ignore her father.

Nora and the kids would have plenty of money to live on from the sale of the company and based on the success I expected with Shu Ling's films, I saw myself a wealthy movie producer.

Traffic stalled while I sat in the Tunnel. Not another blackout? No, the lights stayed on and the carbon monoxide seeped. I gritted my teeth and tried not to breathe. I sat sucking down noxious exhaust. I was an idiot for even thinking about selling out.

I remembered how in therapy Deborah contended I let my dreams and fantasies overwhelm my good sense. I agreed, laughing a little self-defensively that my fantasies could change my view of life as easily as calcium sulfate coagulated soymilk. Toss a little bit of calcium into a tank of soymilk, make a huge vat of tofu. From a vat of tofu, build a dynamic, world-shaking company. My gift: Take a little fantasy, create a whole new happy world in my mind.

Tofu was real world stuff, Soy to the World come to life. I didn't want to sell out. I'd given it my heart and guts and soul for too long. It wouldn't be worth any real money for maybe five years, but I had a payroll of more than two million dollars. Half the town of Clement was eating sirloin and lobster because of American Tofu. When I received a New York Entrepreneur of the Year award, I think I blew all the town fathers' minds. Now everybody in the Chamber of Commerce wanted me to speak or sit on their boards.

Now I had Shu Ling's documentary movie to promote me. Once she released it, I'd be a star of an industrial film. What better way to become known as the Henry Ford of tofu? I'd started with nothing and put tofu into the stomachs of millions. Who else can say that? Besides, who remembers the name of the producer of last year's big bucks blockbuster?

Bottom line? I was the boss now and I planned to stay the boss but what really pissed me off was that again, I had to make a choice between love and money. Between magical sex and vast power. Shu Ling or American Tofu.

I stewed in the cancerous vapors under the Hudson, the power of my anger infusing my muscles like a steroid. If Genevieve wanted to quit, let her. I'd find somebody else, somebody more beautiful, more charming. Maybe a woman who didn't have a kid so she could travel more often, really put American Tofu on the map. I could afford to pay somebody twice what she made, if I had to.

When the traffic finally moved and released me from the fumes of hell, I called Shu Ling to change our meeting back to her apartment. Instead of breaking up with her, I'd persuade her to give me one of her mystical lovemaking sessions. She didn't answer but she'd changed her voicemail message to say she'd see me uptown. I cruised up Tenth Avenue to the hotel.

I had time to shower and change before Shu Ling rang me in my room.

"Hi, Charlie. I'm here. Meet me in Hannigan's downstairs." "Why don't you come up? I booked a beautiful suite, one of the best views in the house."

"Not now. I thought you had something big-time to talk to me about."

"It's changed. I think we have more fun things to do than talk." She laughed. "Crazy like always. I'll wait in the bar."

I spotted Shu Ling at a table in the back of the bar, her headphones on, eyes closed, nodding to the beat.

A gorgeous animal, a sleek feline beast. Slow down, Charlie. Savor the feast.

I slipped past the bar and stopped to soak up her beauty. She was radiant in a tight black silk blouse and her trademark crimson leather pants. Half the men in the place were ogling her. Sensing me, she removed her headphones, stood up and hugged me. We sat beside each other and she pointed to the glass of wine she'd ordered for me.

"Your favorite. A California Merlot. Guess the brand."

I had no idea but when she said, "Gosling," a smile as wide as the Hudson flowed across my face: A witty reference to her message on my voicemail after our *Marmoset* session, when she called me "Little Gander." I settled in for an evening appetizer of repartee and teasing. I was sure a sexual feast of "Orangutan Toes" was on the menu for the night.

"I'm glad you came to the city, Charlie."

"Me, too."

"You got my message?" she asked.

"Which one? I forgot to check my voicemail. I had a lot on my mind." Thirsty, I gulped my wine.

"We're still telepathic then. I called your office this morning." "What about?"

"Let's take a walk. I can't talk seriously in a bar, can you? Besides, you're too cute sitting there." She laid some cash on the table and stood up. "I like you without a mustache. I almost want to kiss your lips."

That she noticed I'd shaved off my mustache, and liked it, lifted my spirits more than anything since the last time I saw her. Shu Ling really paid attention to me.

I congratulated myself for my decision to let Genevieve go her way. I'd devote myself even more to loving Shu Ling and, at the same time, doing whatever I had to to save my company.

"Let's go," she said.

I squeezed beside her into the same compartment of the bar's revolving door and said "I've been thinking about our training program."

"Yeah?"

"I remembered an ancient technique, too. Goes way back."

"You can't be serious," Shu Ling said. "You never heard of Monkey Love before I told you."

"This is so ancient, so embedded in everybody's mind, we all know it. Only when you apply it to Monkey Love, you get the most erotic thrill."

"I doubt it."

"Quick lesson?"

"In public?"

"Nobody but us will know." I leered at her.

"Go ahead."

Waiting on the curb for the light to change, I stuck my tongue out at her. She wrinkled her face and tucked her chin in, wondering what I was up to. I stuck it out again. She didn't respond so I stuck it out once more and got the result I wanted: She stuck her tongue out at me, flipping and tasting the chill evening air again and again with her glistening pink tongue.

"That's it! You got it. See what I told you: everybody knows." "Knows what, you crazy man?"

"Monkey see, monkey do. Now we go to bed and work on the kinks."

Shu Ling grinned. She grabbed my arm and tugged me across the street and we started uptown. The stores on the upper West Side sparkled with pre-Thanksgiving decorations and early Christmas lighting. Cold breeze blew steadily against us as we walked arm in arm up Broadway in the romantic evening twilight, belying how unsettled I felt. My nervousness forced me to keep wagging my tongue.

"After that, I have another one. Learned it from my mother." "What? Get serious. Monkey Love is not perverted. The opposite: it's holy."

"So's this. Goes along with Orangutan Toes. Like this." I maneuvered us to the brick wall of the building and stopped. "I don't know if Chinese do this, but every kid born in this country knows it by heart. All we have to do is add our little erotic spin to it: Imagine I'm holding your bare foot in one hand and your toe in my other."

"As long as I don't have to take off my boots out here. It's cold."

"Here we go. Eenee, meenee, minee, mo, catch a monkey by the toe, If she hollers, make her pay, fifty kisses every day." I tried to kiss her but she averted her face and laughing, pushed me back and started walking.

"Charlie, you're goofy. I really like you. Sometimes you feel like my little brother."

I chuckled. "Hold it, Shu Ling. First of all, I'm older than you. Second, if that's how you treat brothers in China, no wonder you have such a population problem."

Grinning, she slapped me on the shoulder.

"Not that. I mean, how you respect me. How what I do impresses you. How you listen to me. How you trust me to try what I tell you to do."

"I told you I love you. Isn't that how a lover acts? Not just a little brother." I purposely let a hurt note shadow my voice.

"What I mean is, I have a couple of things to tell you and I don't want you to get mad. I want to stay friends."

I stopped in the middle of the sidewalk and turned her toward me. An old man in a shabby ankle-length coat bumped into my back, bounced off, and swore. My Chinese princess and I stood there, staring into each other's eyes. Here it comes, I thought, more bad news. What the hell.

"Let's keep going," I said. "It's easier to talk." We crossed the street between stalled cars. "Well," I said after strolling a block in silence and growing anxiety, "tell me."

"Real fast. Here goes," she said. "The film's off, at least the American Tofu part. And we can't see each other anymore."

I stopped again and stepped around, turning to face her. Speechless, I examined her eyes for the real meaning behind what she said. I saw moist anthracite pupils and yellow streetlight glints, but nothing deeper.

I'd made up my mind two hours before to fight for her in spite of the investigation, Nora, Buhrman, Genevieve, every possible obstacle a man could have. Now she was dumping me: No more Taoist sex, no Henry Ford of tofu movie, no future. Anger hissed into my voice.

"What the fuck do you mean? Do you know what it's cost me to help you make that film? I gave you thousands of dollars of my time...my company's time. I spread the word around the whole industry. Everybody knows I'm in on it. I'll look like an idiot."

"Sorry, Charlie. I can't help it."

"You can't help it."

"Either I pull American Tofu from the movie or ditch the whole project. My backers in Taiwan think all the bad publicity you've had will ruin the film." She kept her face turned away as she talked.

"I'll back your film myself, Shu Ling. It can't cost that much more."

"They're my distributors, too. They control the film."

When I didn't say anything, she stammered, "I can leave the AT footage in, and the shots of the water and the countryside, and say something like 'a typical American-run tofu factory...' That way, if everything blows over, we can change the soundtrack to identify your place."

"IF it blows over! IF it blows over!" I shouted over again and again, charging ahead, feeling the savage freedom of shouting on a New York street. Two or three pedestrians stopped to watch my performance but most put their heads down and trudged on. I turned circles on the sidewalk, waving my arms and shouting "IF, IF!"

I jumped up on the skirt of a light pole like some soap actor and grabbing the pole in both hands, I swung around and around. "If. If. If."

Shu Ling retreated to a storefront doorway and stared at me, giving me plenty of room, but she didn't run away. I stumbled down and climbed up on the bumper of a parked car, then higher, onto the trunk, then the roof. I didn't know what I was doing but it felt good to move and climb and ignore the rules. A guy came out of one of the stores and screamed, "Hey asshole. Get the fuck off my car. I'm gonna beat the shit outta ya."

I scrambled down and tripped off the sidewalk into the gutter, ignoring traffic. A horn blared as a taxi sped past inches from my outstretched hand and shocked me awake. I jumped back and found Shu Ling standing in the middle of the sidewalk, my true love, my betrayer, my teacher, my friend, shaking her head sadly as if she wouldn't be surprised if I tried to kill myself by falling into the grille of a speeding Yellow Cab.

Shu Ling circled my arm with hers. "You're acting like a chimpanzee. Don't be so melodramatic."

"That's me. Charlie the Chimp." I tried to jerk loose, but she held me firmly, turning us back into the uptown pedestrian flow. "No," I said. "Charlie the Chump. That's what Monkey Love does for me."

I resisted her until she leaned into me, tightening her fingers around my biceps. She absorbed my anger into her little body. My agitation began to subside and we walked silently for several blocks, her arm clutching mine as if we were lovers savoring recent love-making, unable to detach our bodies, or anticipating a night of intimacy that we'd begin with a slow stroll in each other's arms.

My mind calmed down and I put my arm around Shu Ling and dismissed my worries, enjoying what was probably my last date with her, at least until I figured out the next steps. I loved her and I knew she cared for me, in her little rich girl way, but my fantasies of a future unencumbered by my own baggage and hers looked really silly right then.

Still, I was in so deep with the Meng family, I had to salvage whatever I could from this bizarre twist of fate. By the time we reached Seventy-second Street, my well-oiled businessman's problem-solving mode kicked in and I realized that the movie itself played a minor role in my plans for expanding American

Tofu. When the fiasco settled down, Shu Ling would name American Tofu in the film, so I might as well wait.

Knowing when not to do something, and not doing it, is as important as knowing when to do it.

Wising up, Chuck? It's not too late. Maybe you can still change your fate.

We stopped at the light in front of the tropical green facade of Gray's Papaya Juice and Hot Dog store at the hectic intersection of Amsterdam and Broadway. I stepped away from Shu Ling and pulled her out of the pedestrian crush. Hoping I'd wrung the self-pity out of my voice, I said, "Why are you dumping me? That's the last thing I expected today. You hugged me, ordered that Gosling wine, walked arm in arm. I've never understood you. Do you really mean it?"

"I don't want to, Charlie. We'd never be able to have a true love the way you want it anyway. We're from two different worlds but we can still be friends." She pulled my hands from her shoulders and held them in her gloved ones.

As my fingers brushed the silky leather on her palms, I grinned. "What about *Tamarin* Toes? Maybe some *Monkey See, Monkey Do?*" Unfortunately, I humored myself more than her.

"That's over." She dropped my hands and shrugged her shoulders. "We can't see each other anymore."

"Who says?"

"My father."

I jammed my fists into my coat pockets. "I knew it. You're still under his thumb."

Meng sliced you, your business, your future. Time to close up the cut and tighten the suture.

His power reached into every single aspect of my life, whether he knew it or not, and I wouldn't be surprised if he did.

"Charlie, you don't get it. If I don't stop seeing you, you won't have your business. Not with him. Not with the others. He doesn't want me associated with you at all."

"Can't you stand up to him? I'm not afraid of him. Or Giordano. My business doesn't depend on them." My bravado sounded hollow even to me. I'd already given up but I couldn't show her how easily I'd been beat, then she stunned me again.

"My father didn't appreciate that article you published about the snake bar. A Taipei paper picked it up and printed it. Now my father's friends in Taiwan are laughing at him for bringing a crude American into their circle."

"I erased Meng Produce from the article."

"Everybody knows who you are over there. They keep track of who my father hangs out with. He's famous in their politics and the food business. He doesn't like the attention you bring him."

The story was my lead-off public relations article for the Soy to the World campaign. I thought I'd written it with panache and humor and respect for tradition, good P. R. for everybody.

"Not only that, your police chief's taken his snooping around to new levels. He asked my father if he was hiding the man who killed your worker. He threatened to call in federal agents to search the premises."

So, that was it. Meng hadn't rejected me only because I'd fallen for Shu Ling and might have an entree into his empire, he had his own big problem. He was hiding something foul and the Chief's stubborn nose had sniffed it out. "Yeah, I know. Meng told me Chinese don't do business the way American companies do. They have their own rules."

"That's right. You know why my father traveled with you to Taiwan?"

I waited but at that point I didn't really care what other excuse she'd make. My stomach rumbled and I almost asked her if she wanted a hot dog, normally, the last thing I would eat.

Shu Ling didn't notice my distraction. She plowed on with her story and though I was curious, I doubted she'd tell me the truth.

"He wanted to see if he could trust you," she said, "maybe let you in on his importing business."

"I know about that," I said. "I've never told anyone anything. I had my suspicions, but I don't know any details."

"The aphrodisiacs? The monkey brains? The bear balls and livers he pays Canadian trappers for? The deer penises he buys from hunters in upstate New York?"

"What? I thought it was mostly ginseng and maybe some rhino horn." Just as I'd suspected: Canada.

"Ginseng is the cover. They all want ginseng but the mainland Chinese are spending millions more for the animal parts. So much of the money they get for making cheap computers and things go for aphrodisiacs. Why do you think my father was such a foe of the Tian An Men Square leaders? They shut down his trade for a year. The Americans tightened import regulations and we lost millions."

'We' she said. She's Meng Produce, too. What an idiot, you. It was always obvious and you ignored it. Take what you can and hoard it.

"Charlie, I like you. I trust you. My father trusts you a lot, really. You've always treated me like a princess, so I'm going to tell you something you can never tell anyone."

Meng had set up this whole conversation. Now, Shu Ling had sweetened me up with her sincerity and flattery, she'd bring on the Big Lie, the falsehood Meng could 'trust' me with, because it didn't matter who I told. I could play, too.

"Once I tell you, you'll know why we can't see each other again. If you want the truth, you've got to promise."

"What? Your father's a sex slave runner?"

"Shut up, Charlie. Don't be an idiot. He's a good man. You know it. He's important. He saves people's lives. And he never wants credit for what he does. But—"

"I don't believe that." My bitterness spilled out. He'd just about ruined my life now.

"No, Charlie. You'll see."

At the green light, we crossed and walked north on Broadway, where she let me take her hand. I inhaled deeply, calming myself. The air across the street smelled strangely fresh, despite the evening traffic.

"Do you want to have dinner, at least?" I asked her. "Great sushi on the next block?"

"How can you even think of eating? But it's a good idea to stop for a minute."

I had no idea she was so upset. She pulled us into the alcove of an unlit storefront. I squinted through the windows and saw stepladders and paint buckets and boxes littering the floor.

"You're shivering, Charlie. It's not that bad."

Hunching over in my topcoat, I said, "It's more important to me than you know, Shu Ling."

"You can't tell anyone this. If you do, and my father finds out? I don't know what he'll do. If I tell you, will you keep quiet? Forever?"

"Forever's a long time. I'll have to think about it." Standing so close to her, I felt desperate and I couldn't keep an idiotic grin off my face.

"Stop playing with me, Charlie." She grabbed my coat collars. "I'm offering you the truth you always wanted. My father trusts you a lot. That's why he sent me to you, remember? But now, he can't afford to be involved with your destiny."

"Sounds like philosophical bullshit." She scowled, probably teasing me again. I'd listen and decide later what to say or what to believe. "All right. I'll keep it quiet, if it's so secret."

Shu Ling lowered her voice. "My father imports human organs. They're harvested from executed prisoners and other people. I think sometimes people sell their organs just to survive. Rich Americans who can't wait in the national transplant queue buy them. Livers, kidneys, lungs, everything. He keeps then in a special refrigerated room at Hunts Point. He says it's a logistics nightmare."

"Jesus! Is that legal?" I stiffened up and backed a step away.

"It's legit, totally safe," she said, letting me go. "I don't think the laws have been made yet. He works with the big pharmaceutical companies. Merck, Roche, doctors from Harvard, doctors from the University of Heidelberg, geneticists from Oxford and Stanford. He provides a service that saves lives. He's part of an international team that's decades ahead of ordinary medical practice, but it has to be under the radar."

"If it's only executed prisoners, that's probably okay. What kind of crimes did they commit? I heard people are executed just for their parts? Someone in the government must know about this," I began to feel numb. If the Chief found out, he'd find some way to implicate me in the organ business, too. Guilt by association.

Meng the murderer. Greer the corpse robber.

"I heard Chinese gangsters killed innocent young people for their body parts. Many families have babies just to sell them."

"That has nothing to do with my father. The people who supply the organs are what Americans call 'criminals,' but in China they're businessmen," she said. "My family has to pull together now, all because of your police chief and your big mouth. Soy to the World is getting too much publicity."

"Hey, Soy to the World helps everybody. It heals people!"

She glowered at me. "Meng Produce has a lot more to lose than you do. My father's friends could get in trouble, and he'd have to call in some big favors. You know my father. He doesn't like owing anybody anything. You'd end up getting investigated, too. Do you want that on top of everything else?"

I rolled my eyes.

"Do you want to be responsible for people losing their lives?"

"What do you mean?" I couldn't resist blowing on my hands and stamping my feet. Doing something, hunching down into my chest, warming my hands, somehow protected me.

"You're so dense." Shu Ling's voice began to break. "Without Meng Produce, dozens of people will die every year. If the cops investigate, the newspapers start mucking around in the governor's family, senators."

"Oh." How big was this?

"He saves lives, Charlie It's totally ethical, but it's got to be secret. America has a whole bunch of primitive laws and all those Christians who think anything with a neo-cortex and a shriveled penis is a saint. Remember the southern senator who supported that abortion doctor killer? That decrepit old senator who had the emergency kidney transplant? My father risked his life to get the kidney to that man. If he ever gets caught, he could go to jail and lose everything."

I stared at her.

"Charlie, just think about it. China executes more people than any other country."

"Yeah, except the U.S."

"No, China has lots more. You don't hear about them, that's all. They're criminals. The only good thing they've ever done with their lives is to give up their organs."

"Jesus, Shu Ling. Your dad must make a lot of money in this business." Tofu meant nothing to him. It was a front.

"Sure. He's a businessman, this is bio-tech. Imagine the delicacy of the surgery, the storage, the shipment, all the details. The timing has to be perfect."

"I guess you can't put a dollar sign on a life," I said. As we walked silently, I thought about the executed, and I was beginning to see Meng's point. This was how he had become so powerful. As long as Congress had an inside track to the organs, the government would never pass trade laws condemning China's human rights abuses. Meng was a master. The Henry Ford of organ transplants. I choked off a laugh. "You're sure the organs come only from prisoners?"

"Of course," she said.

Was she pleading or only trying to persuade me?

"It's only prisoners...convicted criminals, evil people. I told you my father runs an ethical, legitimate business. My father and his colleagues help keep the criminal element under control, both countries."

"In more ways than one," I said, suddenly more nervous than I'd been when I signed my first bank loan. "So this is 'The Special Fruit Company'."

"The what company?"

"Never mind." Whatever name Meng's organ importing company went by, now I understood why "The Special Fruit Company" sounded so hilarious to him and his cronies when I had dinner with them in Taipei.

Shu Ling kept quiet for a minute, then she laced her fingers into mine and gave me Meng's three demands and three offers.

"We have to stop seeing each other."

"What? At all?"

"At all."

I smirked. "I figured that. I'm too close for his comfort."

"Listen. If anybody asks, you don't know me."

"Everybody knows we did the film together. My whole town, half the tofu world. We had our picture in the Clement paper." "Professional's no problem. Personally I mean."

"Did you tell your father we did *Lemur Lips*?"

"Shut up, Charlie. This is not the time to fool around."

"I know, I know. I'm serious."

"Last thing. If anybody asks about your trip to Taipei, you tell them it was business and a cultural tour and you barely saw him."

"That's easy, 'cuz it's true." At that point I leered at her and tried to lick her ear. She stiff-armed me with both of her hands on my shoulders.

"You're acting so stupid."

"How else should I act?" I said. "This whole thing is ridiculous."

Shu Ling shook her head and blinked. "It'll sink in. You were a lot of fun and you did give me a lot of help on the film. I told my father you deserved a lot of credit."

"That's for goddam sure and not only your movie. I gave him the best of everything for seven years. I treated him like a friend, not a customer."

"He likes you."

She said that as if offering me a rare jewel, as if it could replace my dream.

"Business as usual. He'll keep selling your tofu, help you get some new customers, too. He'll ignore your Chief's insults, and he'll send out word to try to find Chen."

The full impact of her message settled in: Meng and I were done except for routine business. He'd never buy the company and I'd never be welcomed into the inner circle of power in the international produce world. Maybe I no longer wanted into that circle anyway. "What if I want to keep seeing you? What if I don't agree to all these conditions?"

"My father can't predict what might happen. He's protecting both of us, Charlie. Don't you get it?"

It was brilliant. Meng gave me no choice. A light as cold and pulsing as the black lights in the Taipei "barbershop" filled my head. I held Shu Ling and kissed her hard and long. I told her I loved her and I always would and, grinning, I guaranteed I'd see her again because she owed me an *Orangutan Toes* lesson.

"You agree, Charlie?"

"It's over with us, Shu Ling, but...who knows?" I flagged down a cab and put her in it. Before I closed the door, I said "Too bad your dad couldn't get everyone in congress a brain transplant."

She laughed. "No, but Denzel Washington's people have inquired about other parts."

"Sure," I said, waving good-bye and hustling back to the Empire Hotel.

Forget the Monkey Toes. You may love her, but you gotta let her go.

I began to mentally dismiss Shu Ling from my life. People who let me down, no matter how much I liked them before, they can evaporate,for all I care.

Shu Ling didn't really betray me, but Gen was amazingly accurate.

Shu Ling led you by your nose, your ears, mostly by the thing between your legs, the thing that grows.

Yeah, it was true. She used my lust to get what she wanted. She was always in her father's shadow and I was too drunk on my lust to see.

She didn't have anything I wanted now. For God's sake, I wasn't about to get into the human meat business. "Tofu: The Meat of the Fields" was as close I was going to come to being any kind of a meat distributor, I don't care how many lives I'd save as Meng's partner. How many would I have to take? Jesus.

Took you long enough to figure out what it's really all about.

If letting Shu Ling go was all I had to do I was glad to be free of Meng's schemes, as long as he kept ordering tofu every week and paying us on time. In the long run, it didn't matter much that Shu Ling and I were history.

***

Once I crossed the George Washington Bridge and headed north on the I-87 with the other late-evening commuters milling toward home, a state of calm settled over me. I stopped for gas and something to eat at the rest area just south of Albany. Ironically, after our exchange in front of the hot dog shop on Broadway, I gravitated to the hot dog stand.

I ordered the first hot dog I'd eaten in at least ten years, slathered it with mustard, and I sat down at the bar to eat. I loved it. I'd tried quite a few tofu hot dogs, but one bite of a real hot dog, and I knew the only way you could make tofu taste that good would be to add pig fat and sugar. So, what's the point? Cook tofu the way it's supposed to be, the old-fashioned Asian way, and when you want a hot dog, eat a real one.

Invigorated, I got back on the highway and set the cruise control at seven miles above the speed limit. The traffic was so light I leaned back and almost entered an alpha state. Sometimes I have to talk to myself out loud to know what I'm thinking or feeling.

I started a conversation with Meng that changed my whole attitude toward life.

'Meng, you old bastard. All I wanted was true love and you repossessed the only woman I really loved in the last five years. Yeah, I loved Becky, but our future would have been so crazy.

I'll admit it to you, she was a stand-in for Shu Ling, and now you've ripped her away. You broke my heart, old man.'

I listened as hard as I could, but he kept quiet.

'I know, you had to do it. You didn't really mind the article but the Chief is getting too close. He's a clever son of a bitch, isn't he? Brighter than we thought. Shu Ling and I were getting closer in a different way. But you have too much to lose. Your big secret. So you told me your big secret. Why?'

That's when I got it. Meng had given me something far richer than even the hand of his girl, a revelation a thousand times bigger and far more perilous than my little secret about Becky.

Meng maneuvered through his days at Hunts Point as if the organ smuggling business didn't exist, pretending he was a vegetable trader, keeping up an impeccable front, while fielding immense pressure from some of the most powerful people in the world. No doubt earning enormous profits.

His life wasn't so different from what I was up to, only we lived on different levels. His Special Fruit Company saved a few rich people's lives in the short run by providing them with healthy organs. I saved millions of peoples' lives over the long term by providing healthy food, not the poisons the mainstream food industry foists on people.

Who's got the most to lose? Meng or you? You choose.

As I stacked up our similarities and differences, at first it seemed that Meng did have a lot more to lose if the wrong people discovered his secret. In terms of money, yes, but family, self-esteem, reputation? Not really. In fact, he had more protection than I'd ever muster, more powerful friends, more options. In reality, I could lose everything if my secret came to light. And, worse, compared to him, I had far less to gain. He'd already entered the inner sanctum of the global untouchables.

By forbidding Shu Ling to see me, he'd severed our emotional ties and turned any future Meng and I had into strictly business. The truth was, now that I'd attained maybe my first rational view of him since I knew him, I saw that our entire history had been strictly and only business. Shu Ling was a wild card that the old man flipped out of the deck.

But, and this was amazing, when he ordered Shu Ling to tell me about the organ trade, he had Shu Ling tell me because it had never come up between Meng and me personally, and he could deny everything.

Meng would never know it, but by letting me know about the organ importing, he revealed how I could handle my secret: Live life the way I wanted to, ignore what society demands, don't ask permission. Meng had shown me the path to reaching my dream of freedom.

I drove home in a state of euphoria, fearless and eager, arriving in Clement at one a.m., focused, a man of mission. Meng's secret alchemized in my heart, radiating the power to change the chaos of my life into the pure gold of power.

Chapter Ten

Genevieve

GRACE UNDER PRESSURE OF DESIRE

Before I met with Gianni to ask for his help with finding a new job, I hadn't made love to a man since I sent Benko packing.

In my lonely musings, a storm of memories about men rolls over me, confusing one with another. One's long blonde hair curling on a bald brown one's neck. One's deep laugh roaring out of another thin chest, sauntering athletic hips angling toward me.

My imagination conjures these apparitions into my life where they surround me, offering me their airy love, their ghostly touches precisely on my perfect pleasure points, their pure attention until I wake out of my trance, unmoved, sick of their perfection, sick of creating spirit lovers to guide my hands over my body, resenting their ghostliness, grieving because I needed self-deluding sorcery.

It's their silence I can't bear. Beautiful, precise images I can summon, but sounds? As soon as I magicked my shadow men into speech, noise emerged from their mouths like ghoulish moans or dull commands that never found the shapes or tones that make sense.

Yet my dream-men satisfy me with their faithfulness, their loyalty to my desires. The men-in-bodies in my life always disappoint me. They're inconsistent in their affections and confused about their feelings. They all go by the same name: Mr. Ambivalence. They act muddled about whether they can love me as freely as they love, or hate, their mothers; mixed-up about whether they love me or love themselves in my loving them, they have to follow rules and parameters to know who they are. Even the rebels and bohemians I've loved spend most of their energy in just another kind of obedience, proving to themselves the authorities have no control over them.

Even before the Chief scared me off, I'd begun to seek a graceful way out from Benko. I had to work too hard to ignore his boring narcissism and crude physicality. He and I didn't find much to talk about beyond work, food, and sex. As much as I loved and craved them all, Benko hadn't had a new thought or made an original move in weeks. He, his mind, and even that spectacle of a sausage began to bore me, and boredom depressed me far more than loneliness.

Buhrman's investigation gave me a good excuse to hang up my memories of Benko along with the photos in my 'Boyfriend Gallery,' a show nobody but me would ever see. There, the pictures I'd taken of his inimitable appendage would take their place among the other shots I'd taken of other men to portray rare gifts each of my lovers had given me.

Once I stopped seeing Benko regularly, he turned volatile and unpredictable. For a while, he completely stopped speaking to me in person. When I'd ask for help fetching samples or marketing materials from the warehouse, he'd walk up to me, thrust his eyes two inches away from mine and glare at me, breathing stale garlic into my face. He'd grunt and turn around and walk away, his neck muscles twitching.

Then, when I felt relief that he'd given up on me, he'd call. I'd lead him on, assuring him that I was still fond of him, always reminding him that he had to treat me right if he wanted to keep my friendship. I let him believe that after the investigation, he and I could rekindle our affair.

He ignored the implication that I might not want him.

"I want you always, Genevieve. I want you now. You make me too crazy to wait. But I'll be good. Damn Chief. Maybe something happens to him."

"Benko. Don't be stupid."

"Just play. Make you laugh. Too serious. Let's have fun."

"It's not easy, Benko. Best we take it easy like we agreed." "Sure, boss. When you say yes, my word is always yes. Don't know if I can control myself, Gen. I want you too bad."

"That's not 'friends.'"

"Friends need love. You need me."

"Benko, I'm gonna hang up."

He barked "No. Friends now. Later, later we go back to lovers."

I wanted to believe him, but I couldn't. Every once in a while, I called him. Telephone check-ins with Benko became my shield. A flimsy protection, but by talking to him now and then, I counted on being able to detect any overt hostility and keep him at bay. If I couldn't, I didn't know what I'd do.

***

In the airport the day Charlie revealed his affair with Shu Ling, I punched in Giordano Brothers' number. Gianni was out.

"I'm boarding a plane right now," I told his secretary. "I need his help with something. Have him call me as soon as he can. It's not urgent. He knows my number."

Once I made the call to Gianni for help, he reappeared in my emotional consciousness. With no other man to absorb my affection, my energy naturally flowed to reflecting on our time together. It had been more than six months since we slept together. So much had happened I barely understood where Gianni fit into my life any more.

Once, he told me he'd never loved a woman for her mind before me, and it was the hottest love he'd ever felt. When we separated so abruptly last spring, I wanted to kill him. My jealous mind seethed with every kind of revenge.

My favorite vengeance fantasy was watching the Berkshire house on fire, burning all the memories stored in the sheets, the couches, everywhere we made love. I could see that poor polar bear we'd lain on in front of the fireplace snarling as the place collapsed in flames.

During the first weeks of separation, I wrote Gianni letters and emails cursing him, but I never mailed them. I dialed his home number in Brooklyn at least ten times, always hanging up when anyone answered—it was always his wife or kid. In late April, I bought a dozen long-stemmed red roses and dried them in my oven. I wrapped the crisp, burnt petals in red silk, and mailed it to his office. His reply a few days later: A birthday bouquet with a sweet note. Of course he loved me—six months ago.

A week after I called him from Philadelphia, Gianni called. With typical grace, he apologized. "I'd have called from Buenos Aires if my secretary had forwarded your message. You know that."

That morning, I got out of bed with laryngitis. I could barely whisper. "I believe you, Gianni." My throat burned when I spoke, but I had to talk to him. "I have to talk to you, Gianni," I croaked. "As soon as possible."

"Right now," he said.

"I can barely talk. How about next Monday?"

"I'm coming to the Berkshires tomorrow, for the weekend. Alone. Do you want to meet met there?"

I knew what would happen if I met him there alone and I wanted it. "Are you sure? I just want to talk business."

"That's fine. It's better to talk business without any pressure. We'll just relax. You sound like you need a rest, anyway."

How can I relax with you? I thought. You'll just drive me out of my mind.

I mumbled, "I'm still mad at you."

"Good. You still have feelings for me."

"Forget it. That was a long time ago, Gianni."

"I have a perfect memory. With you, yesterday is the same as today to me."

"Tomorrow is different," I said. "I need your help and friendship, that's all."

"Anything, Genevieve. You know that."

We decided to meet at his home on Saturday noon for lunch. I told him that I needed to leave by three and that he should keep his chef on duty. "Being with you alone scares me, Gianni."

"I'm a bear cub."

"You don't understand how vulnerable I am."

"I'll be good, I promise. You're the one…"

I laughed. "We're both the one, so you better be good."

Protecting myself from reviving my deepest feelings for him, I concocted an escape plan. I would arrange to pick up Liam early that night so if I had to run from temptation, I could plea lack of childcare. If I was tempted to give in to the urge I'd feel on the skin of my thighs for the touch of the hair on his legs, I'd get in my car and drive away because I had to fetch Liam.

With Liam happy and safe at Joanne's with her son Nelson, my mind and heart were free for once.

Like the first time I stepped through the front door of his Berkshire home, the moment we looked into each other's eyes, probing to learn what depths we'd allow each other, we disappeared into our enchanted mountain hideaway.

I'd mistaken Gianni's flirtation on the phone for superficial toying with our love. Inside the front door of his house, he drew me to him, kissing me delicately, almost shyly and I let myself fall against him, opened my mouth, hugged his body so tightly I felt him tremble.

"Genevieve, darling. Sweet Genevieve," he whispered, pulling back. "It hasn't really been six months. I feel like we just held each other yesterday."

He led me to the couch where we sat in front of an applewood fire, holding hands, staring into the flames.

The voice I'd regained chunks of that morning melted away again as I relaxed. For the first time in months, I felt safe. American Tofu, Charlie, the dead woman, Buhrman, Benko, my photos and cookbook, all the work seemed like minor scenes in an old movie. I felt I was home with Gianni and I dropped all my fears about losing myself in him. I didn't care what happened.

I gazed around the study, realizing for the first time I was a foreigner to this world, an interloper from the world of work. His riches surrounded us: the marble mantle with gold and crystal candlesticks ranked across it, the black and mahogany leather chairs and couch squatting like waiting pack animals, the slim lamps shining warm light through chafed cotton shades. I felt like I was in a movie set. I was the star playing the pretty servant girl he'd sneaked into the mansion when everyone else was gone.

"You want to talk?" Gianni asked. "No, don't answer."

I couldn't speak louder than a dull whisper anyway.

He scrolled through his music collection. In a moment, mellow saxophone notes surrounded us.

"Old Miles," he said. "*Love songs.*" He handed me a snifter of blackberry brandy. "This will cure you, if anything can."

I grinned, mouthing, "Family collection?" His family in Naples produced an elderberry liqueur that Gianni claimed tasted like the blood of resurrected Christ. I sipped it and as the creamy elderberry juice slipped down my throat, the alcohol vapors rose into my head and I almost swooned.

"In heaven yet? Take another sip."

"I'm afraid I'll never make it all the way up there," I rasped. "Way too sinful."

Mocking an amorous priest, he caressed my hand and whispered, "All can be forgiven, my child."

I watched him stir the embers and add several fragrant logs to the fire.

"It hasn't been easy, Genevieve," he said as he refilled our glasses. "I tried to be out of the office every time you came near Hunts Point. I feel so much for you, I often wanted to cash in, pick you up, take you off to Fiji. In my dream, we live the rest of our lives in paradise."

He stood up and paced in front of the fireplace. The chill November sun dropped in through the windows, stretched across the carpet, and climbed into my lap. At least he was opening up to me but I couldn't let him take control of us. I needed a simple little thing—his help getting a new job quick—if he couldn't help, so be it.

I watched the sizzling fire, listening to logs shift and fall, like American Tofu and my whole life in Clement, weakened and surrendering to the insistent flames that, once started, would have to burn themselves out.

"Let's have lunch," he said. "I'm the chef."

I swallowed the last of my liqueur and whispered, "You weren't supposed to give your man the afternoon off."

Gianni pulled me off the couch and led me into the kitchen. "I couldn't help it. On weekends, he works at his brother's shop in Lenox."

"Likely story."

"But true. He'll be home by five, and we have a lot to do, so," raising his eyebrows and winking, "we have to hurry."

He wasn't referring to getting lunch over with or discussing my new job. Heat from the liqueur rose up from my stomach into my face.

"You look like a Christmas cherub with your cheeks all red and shiny like that." He kissed me on my lips and twirled me into the kitchen where uplifting strings sang from invisible speakers.

"Albinoni," he said. "I can't cook without him." I watched him scramble eggs and tofu with leeks and elephant garlic in an elegant copper pan with the *savoir-faire* of a professional chef.

He tore chunks of bread off a loaf of focaccia and divided the pieces with his fingers. He placed the crusty sandwiches next to tossed salads on white over-sized plates, poured two mugs of coffee, and set our lunch on the counter.

"Mangé," he ordered, "mangé," smiling as if he'd just created a gourmet delicacy for the pope. Or the queen.

We ate in silence, smiling and chewing and swinging our heads and shoulders in time with the music, like casual friends. The kitchen gas fireplace roared, relaxing me even more.

"What a meal. I wish I could make that."

His face lit up and he bowed to his waist.

"You cured me," I said. My voice grated and skipped like an old man's straining to make a point. "My throat doesn't hurt and I can talk a little bit."

"Let's not get serious too soon," he said.

"I already agreed to that, last spring. Remember?" A note of bitterness crept into my halting words.

"Genevieve." He moved toward me. "I'm sorry."

I stepped back. "Gianni, don't confuse me."

"I just want to help," he said.

"It's so hot in here. Can we go for a walk?"

"Good idea." Gianni brought me my coat and said, "I like talking among my trees. Somehow the words sound deeper."

I saw him in a new way, as handsome and mature as ever, but he acted less sure of himself. He moved tentatively around me, as if he didn't know how to treat me without cues, as if he'd forgotten my body language.

Strolling in the cool sunlight, past fields dotted with fat, golden pumpkins, we lingered in the apple orchard and plucked mushy fruit from trees that were all but stripped of their bounty.

"Apple wood makes delicious smelling fire, doesn't it? When you have to sacrifice a few trees for the health of the orchard, you don't even think about it."

Standing beside dried corn still not harvested, rustling in the breeze, we marveled at the sky's opalescent blues and the rich harvest his farm offered up so casually.

"I could never leave this," he murmured. "But I have an idea. It might work." He gripped my hand, chafing it to warm it, and we walked on. "You know I love you and respect you as much as anybody in my life. You need a job now. With all the craziness around the accident in your plant, your call didn't surprise me."

"It's been wild," I said.

"Your police chief has visited me twice and Charlie calls me way too often for my comfort. My comfort for you, I mean."

That was the first I'd heard of Buhrman's actual visits to him. I cocked my head, concerned.

"No problems," Gianni went on, responding to my gesture.

"He's just fishing. I like the man. Good country cop, doing his job and having a good time. Poor Greer, though. Buhrman's turned up the pressure on him."

We went back inside to his study. He banked the fire and poured us small snifters of cognac. He raised his glass, "La Vita."

"La Vita."

"Now, what shall we do?" he asked.

"First things first," I said, "like they say in business."

"Absolutely. The only way."

I loved jousting with him, tossing double entendre back and forth. Unlike Benko, Gianni was the Prince of Flirtation. A cloud passed over the sun and the room dimmed, not unexpectedly, at the thought of Benko.

"I'm in a mess. Charlie's acting like an idiot."

"Idiot?"

"Messing around with Meng's daughter, pissing Meng off, freaking out."

"I could tell he's been on edge from his calls."

"I think he's going to lose Meng's trade."

"How serious are he and the girl?"

"It's over."

"Good. She's protected. Meng will be happy now."

"He's going through my files."

"He can, you know. Boss has the right."

"Gianni, who's side are you on?"

"Yours. What do you think? See it from his point of view. He's going through your files because he has to cover his ass, in case you leave."

"I never said anything about leaving. Well, I threatened, but he didn't take it seriously."

"He knows."

"How?"

"He's a good businessman, just covering his ass."

"All right. He's not the only problem."

Gianni sat back his chair and crossed his leg over his knee. Sipping his brandy, he waited.

"The guy I've been seeing since we split up?"

"The Russian. Low class, but what can I say?"

"Worse than that. He's a brute. When the Chief told me he was investigating him along with Charlie in the death? I told him I couldn't see him anymore and he pushed me down on the couch and I thought he would rape me or hit me."

Gianni jumped up from his chair and sat beside me, knee to knee.

"Do not fool around with this guy. He's a powder keg."

"You think? That's the whole point."

"Did you call the police? Do you want me to send somebody up to talk to him? I can."

"No, no. I can handle it. I've got him calmed down. He thinks the Chief has targeted him for murder, so he's keeping his distance from me, for now. But I want to get out of Clement tomorrow."

"Just quit. You can work for me in New York."

"I can't. Liam—"

"Telecommute. Start Monday."

"I can't. I owe too much to Charlie and Nora. I can't leave them like that. Besides, I have to give Liam some time to adjust. He's not a baby any more."

Gianni stood up and banked the fire again. "Are you sure you're safe?" The apple wood crackled and its heart-breaking sweet fragrance drifted into the study.

"Yes. I'm sure," I said, taking a deep breath.

"When do you want to start at Giordano Brothers?"

"Gianni, you're so sweet. I can't go to work for you. It would be pure misery to see you walk by my desk and know..."

He nodded his head and shrugged.

"Remember the guy you mentioned on the West Coast? The guy who did the new foods research?"

"Sure. You want to work for him? That's a long ways away. San Francisco."

He meant that San Francisco was a long way away from him. "I could use a big change."

He observed me for a long time then lay back on the couch and sighed. The leather crinkled and he made himself cozy. "All right."

"Thank you, Gianni. I'll start with him. I don't know what I'll do for sure."

"I can call him and set you up right away."

"Don't. Just give me his number and be my reference. That's all. I don't want to owe you more than I should."

"You won't owe me—"

"Gianni, thank you. Maybe you could give me a list of other names, too? Without mentioning it to anyone? I don't want word to get out that I'm job hunting until after the New Year."

"I'll have Jerrylyn email names of a few people you can trust. That's all?"

"That's all. I wanted to tell you about how scared I've felt lately. I needed to talk to somebody."

He sat up and pulled me to him. "It's all right. It's a big change, but any help you need, I'm here. You know that?"

"Yes." I kissed his ear. You're the sweetest. I only wish..." "Mmmmmm?"

"You know. Can't go there."

"Guess not," he said. "Well, now everything's straightened out? Anything else?"

Raising my eyebrows and tsking my teeth, pretending to think hard. "Not that I can think of." My knees trembled a little and I felt my jaw quiver. The whole front of my body went warm, except my nipples. They swelled and stretched tight against my sweater. Gianni's eyes dropped to my chest.

"You came all the way over here for that?" His voice rose. Even he lost his grace under pressure of desire.

I said, "That and lunch." I shrugged and my nipples hardened further. "You know women. Talking in person makes us feel better." "You feel better now?"

"Much." I kissed him quickly on the lips and then on the nose and stood up.

"Gianni, do you know what an incredible life you have?"

"Yes," he said, standing up and crossing to the liquor cabinet. "You could stay here if you need to get out right away."

"I can't."

"Are you sure? Leave right now and I'll take care of your expenses until you get your new job."

"No. I have to give Charlie plenty of notice. Right now, I think he's on the verge of a nervous breakdown." The last thing I wanted was to take money from Gianni.

"What do you mean?"

"He's gone on a manic work spree. Ten meetings every day about things like bathroom policy. A memo every hour about nothing. He calls up the Chief every time he hears from a consumer and pleads with him to solve the crime or close the case." Talking about Charlie and work again dropped my temperature and I decided to leave.

"A lot of pressure. So far, I think he's done a good job." Gianni paused, gathering his thoughts. "If Charlie can't find anyone to try to fill your shoes...you move on to your new job by spring anyway? He won't complain. I've known plenty of guys like him. They're hard on the outside, they know it all. Inside, they're marshmallows."

I hugged Gianni, brushing his upper lip with a light kiss. I let my lips linger and he kissed back, but sweetly.

"I have to ask you something, Genevieve."

"Oh?"

"What about us?" he asked.

Feeling loose I said, "Que sera, sera. Right?" I touched his hand, raised it to my lips, then settled it over my heart. "Gianni, I know you can't change your life for me. I can't change my life for you either."

I started to feel light-headed. I would be free of American Tofu and Charlie and all the pressures. Gianni would be my friend and that's all I wanted.

"You'll find a new job ten times better than tofu."

"I know I will." I stood and tugged him up beside me, pulling us toward the stairs. "Don't you think we should celebrate?"

"I don't know," he demurred. "You're tired. Besides, you don't have a new job yet."

"Oh. Right. By the way, let's not tell Charlie or anyone until I get the job?"

"Of course not."

I turned, pretending I needed my coat. "Well, Signor Giordano, if we've finished our meeting, I guess it's time for me to leave. I have a child to retrieve from his computer dungeon before he gets captured by the evil terrorists on the tundra."

"Wait, Ms. O'Connor. There is one more aspect of this agreement I think we should work out before you leave. Do you have a moment?" Stepping back, he addressed me, politely, formally, his eyes twinkling. "Would you mind stepping into my private office. It shouldn't take long."

I pretended disappointment and glanced at my watch. "Well, let's make it quick," I whispered.

"I can't promise how quick we'll be. As you know, these important matters often take longer than you expect."

I ran up the steps and he chased me hooting. Stripping quickly in the chilly upstairs room, we slipped between cold sheets. The past, the demands of our present lives beyond the room, our possible futures, sank under our breathing and quiet moans.

I caught Gianni's thick gold necklace in my fingers, tightening it gently around his throat as he wound my hair in his fist, drawing my face into his. He tried to swallow me through my mouth, scissoring my waist and bottom between taut legs, squeezing until my bones ached.

We rolled and kicked and rode the bed like a raft in a storm trying to rip its anchor free from the grip of the rocks down below.

The last of the light sank with us into a place where nothing existed except our lips, our soaked bellies and thighs, the twists and arcs we threw our bodies into as we sought total immersion in each other's moans and laughs.

"You're too sexy when you groan," he said.

Our fingers and tongues swirled everywhere, moist weedy tentacles wrapping around thighs, licking down our necks and shoulders, tugging and tilting us back and forth across the bed.

He turned me on my belly and said, "Ssshhh." I shivered as he poured cool oil along my spine, his fingertips brushing it into the sweat on my back. He kneaded my long muscles, nipping folds of skin between his fingernails, a big cat teasing his willing prey, softening the last bit of tension out of my shoulders.

Pressing his elbows into the sides of my lower back, he elongated the rigid muscles that clung to my hips, then pulling them like taffy, he released the stiffness that thousands of miles of driving had bound like a thick belt around my pelvis.

He rubbed my bottom, gently at first, probing my soft fat with his thumbs, then he began to slap and pinch until I jerked away.

"Ssshhh," he said again. Soothing the warmed skin on my bottom, he continued massaging my thighs and calves. As he lifted my foot, blowing warm breath on my sole and licking the tips of my toes with his soft tongue, I drifted into a spell, floating on a cloud with angel wings nudging me ever higher into ecstasy.

I don't know how long I dozed, but I stirred when I felt Gianni enter me. Both on our stomachs, we lay languorous, our bodies shifting in tiny motions signaling the storm's potential return. As we began to move into each other more quickly, the friction of our bodies as gentle as two wide rivers joining courses, I heard Gianni gasp. A sob broke from his throat and I immediately began weeping. We rolled over and stared deeply into each other's streaming eyes as we continued pushing and pulling, ignoring ourselves, urging the other to climax.

We collapsed into a delicious nap under the eiderdown quilt, twisted into each other like a French braid of arms and legs. We woke and hugged each other as if we were the only people on earth. Then, still without speaking, we dressed and made our way down the softly lit main staircase.

Gianni offered me one last blackberry brandy toast and, handing me a bottle "Just like the pope's," he said. "Don't worry. You'll have the best job of your life."

We hugged like we'd never hug again, and I left. I drove down the narrow lane and pulled over before I turned onto the street, so I could cry.

***

I drove home with my windows wide open to the crisp night and the heater blasting a blanket of heat across my lap. The stars shone so brightly in the glossy sky each one seemed to beam a message to me. Love. Peace. Freedom. A bright new life. Even though I'd long before learned never to count on anything, I let all my worries and fears dissolve in the chilly breeze blowing across my face.

Eventually, my exhilaration faded and I began to feel incredibly sentimental about American Tofu. What an emotional wimp. But AT has changed me more than any other chapter in my life. I loved everybody I worked with, even that rat Benko when he backed off and treated me like a friend, and I would miss all my customer friends. The worst thing about changing jobs and leaving AT was that I didn't know how I'd break the news to Liam. He was finally feeling at home in Clement, happy with friends, winning meets with his swim team.

The other worse thing was that Charlie would hate me for leaving him in the lurch. What did he say? The mice were leaving the ship?

Once he knew about Benko and me, he'd probably fire him, but that wouldn't do me any good. Besides, he couldn't fire Benko before the next Chinese New Year anyway. The Year of the Rooster had his whole Soy to the World dream riding on it. I'd stick with him till we got through that and then, up up and away to San Francisco.

I stopped in front of Joanne's and sat in my car, thinking, before I went in to get Liam.

I had a clear mind for the first time since Becky died. That beautiful sex with Gianni this afternoon cleared my mind.

I did love them all at American Tofu. But I had to admit to myself I was really getting tired of Charlie's antics and Benko's bullying attitude. Trying to control them both was taking way too much out of me.

I wouldn't leave Charlie in the lurch, but if he gave me any trouble about my moving on, I'd walk out. Nora would have to deal with him on her own. And Benko, he's either an idiot in love with himself or a bully who knows only one way to get his way.

I picked up my boy and pulled into our driveway by midnight. I kissed my lovely, patient son good night and tumbled exhausted into my bed for the deepest sleep since Gianni and I first celebrated the Year of the Monkey, nearly a year ago.

Chapter Eleven

Charlie

A RIDE WITH THE CHIEF

blue lights flash, clever
cop angles for a big catch
charlie trout slips away

I came out of my office bathroom after lunch the Wednesday before Thanksgiving to hear my secretary say, "No problem, Chief. His calendar is clear this afternoon. I'll tell him you'll be by at two."

At that moment, the floor leapt up into my face. I closed my eyes and tried to breathe while my body swerved back and forth. I wanted to support my forehead against the wall of carpet, but when I leaned toward it, the carpet backed off, beckoning me to follow it down. Lucky, I stayed almost vertical.

I staggered to my office and collapsed on the couch, planning to lie there until I regained my balance. When I lay down, the vertigo disappeared.

Since I returned from Taiwan, I'd worked myself and everyone else to the bone. If I hadn't ignored the little symptoms of fatigue and stress, I doubt if I'd been able to drive Soy to the World beyond the idea stage. Talking, phoning, writing, following up, turning people on and keeping them fired up wore me out, especially since I was carrying the weight of the investigation on top of work.

I was lucky I didn't have to worry about managing the core of our business: the production. Benko had offered to run the factory, the warehouse, and the shipping department single-handedly. I gave him a nice bonus and let him hire a mechanic to help with maintenance. After his first successful week in charge, I called him into my office.

"Benko, you're saving my ass. I don't have the energy to handle all the details."

"That's fine, Charlie. My job. I do it, everybody's happy."

"Doing it right, too. I see the costs are holding."

"Good. I'm good."

"Here's a little present. We call it a token of appreciation." I handed him a bottle of Stolichnaya.

"You don't have to do that." He pulled the bottle out of its carton and unscrewed the cap. "Here. Old custom. Drink, we share." I drank from the bottle, not too deeply. He drank a long slug.

"Good stuff, Charlie. Only thing, next time. I like scotch. You know single malt? Laphroig? The best." He grinned.

"Sure, Benko," I said, not amused that he wanted a fifty dollar bottle of scotch rather than the twenty five dollar of vodka, but I had to admit he had balls to tell me what he wanted while he assumed there would be a next time. "Just keep up the good work and we'll see."

"Thanks, Charlie. I got it all covered."

"Great, Benko."

"By the way. Another Scotch? The MacAllan. I like it. Ever try it?"

With the way my head felt, if he kept things cool in the factory so I didn't have to think about them at all, I'd buy him a case of single malt scotch.

***

I'd been hungry for Thanksgiving like never before, not the feast, but the time off.

All I wanted was real down-time: raking the yard, taking the kids for a burger and the movies, maybe getting out the old Joy of Sensual Massage workbook with Nora. I usually hiked in the woods to relax, but since Becky died, whenever I'd tried bushwhacking in the trees, everything about her came back and that's the last thing I needed.

As I got out of bed in the morning, dizzy spells would strike. All day, at random, they'd strike. I'd walk to my car and the driveway would spring into my face. Or I'd drive down the block and the car would tilt sideways, and I'd wobble on two wheels, then I'd be fine for maybe a day. Eventually, one of the office ladies said they'd all been talking and they wanted me to take some time off.

"We can handle the business," she said. "You trained us good."

I was touched but I'd stay on deck until the Thanksgiving break even though my body shouted at me loud and clear: Charlie, clean up your act or I'm gonna scrub your insides so pure you'll never stop squeaking.

The one person I didn't want to see that afternoon was Buhrman. We'd already shut down production for the long weekend and the office staff would leave by three. I lay on my office couch preparing for him, resting my eyes.

The Chief was the most punctual man I'd ever met. He marched through the front door precisely at two o'clock. If I wasn't ready exactly on time for a planned meeting with him, he let me know his opinion that my work habits were slovenly and unlikely to ever lead to success. All my employees bowed and scraped before Buhrman as if he alone determined what happened to their futures. But not if I could help it.

From my couch, when I rolled up the blinds, I could see everyone who approached the front of the building. I watched Buhrman near the plate glass door and stop to check his reflection. He pumped up his brass-buttoned chest and tilting his hat back, ambled in like he was the headman.

The way he struts? No wonder you have a knot in your guts.

Once the investigation ended, I intended to do my best to have him demoted or transferred. I'd love to see him humbled in the local newspaper and retired as fast as possible to a parking lot security job in Miami. That afternoon, he pranced around the office like a proud tom turkey, the one who kept his head. His mood worried me.

"Hey, Charlie. Why's it so gloomy in here?"

I'd dimmed all the lights except my screen saver with its migrating flock of winged tofus.

"Let's go," Buhrman said in an unusually friendly tone. "Take a ride in the cruiser. You all right?" He stepped close, peering at my face. "You're pale."

"I'm fine. Just tired." Ignoring the hand he offered, I slipped off the couch and sidestepped him. The spell had passed, leaving me with dampness on my chest and a pain pulsing at the base of my skull. I switched on the overhead lights, trying to dissolve the gloom that had settled into my heart like a permanent November, the month of low skies, low sales, low energy. "I don't really feel like going anywhere," I said. "I was just about to go home for a long weekend. My kids are expecting me. Am I under arrest, or what?"

"Hey. Take it easy. I'm doing a patrol shift this afternoon. Thought you'd enjoy a quiet drive and a nice talk. Clear some things up before we take off for the holiday." He opened the office door, motioning me out.

Resistance would only antagonize him and though I didn't mind making him mad, I sure didn't have the stamina to deal with him the way I wanted to.

It's only a bluff. He knows enough. Show him you're not well. Have a dizzy spell.

As usual, Jiminy made sense. The vertigo might come in handy. Work with whatever you're given, another one of my business success mottos.

As soon as he settled in the patrol car, Buhrman switched on the flashing blue lights.

"In a rush, Aaron?" I asked, annoyed, but not very surprised at his adolescent ostentation. "I thought we're out for a peaceful ride." "That's right. The lights make sure nobody bothers us."

And they make sure that everybody sees us. Buhrman drove slowly, deliberately. The streets were empty, as if everyone had abandoned the neighborhoods to burrow in and wait out a storm. I hadn't seen the weather report.

"I hear you're a pretty good boss?"

He's using the old routine: Doodles and Dips. Gonna open up King Tofu's lips.

Not likely. "I try to be. Like any employer, I have some problem workers. The rest, you trust them and treat them like grown-ups, they like you. They do a better job than if you browbeat them." I kept everything simple with him, so his skeptical mind would miss any dubious claims in my philosophy: if something caught his attention, he'd consider it a clue.

"Yeah. Not like criminals. You have to stand over them all the time or they'll con you and rip you off before you know it." He paused. "You must know your workers pretty well?"

Leading by asking, the oldest sales trick in the book. I'd play along. "Pretty well. We check references. Regular evaluations." "How well did you know the MacDaniel woman?"

Jesus, I thought. He knows. Here it comes. Now I'm fucked. My other voice held its breath. "Not too well. Why?"

"We dug up some interesting new information. Thought you ought be the first to know. The first outside of criminal justice circles, that is."

"About the fingerprints?" I'd turn the tables on the interrogator.

"Naw. Didn't I tell you? No clear leads there. She must have had a doozey of a party. She knew half the people in Clement. You heard about the drug paraphernalia? We expected that, after the blood tests and all."

"Yeah. Wasn't that in the paper?"

Buhrman's image quivered and my stomach began to twist up again. Buhrman's voice developed a faint echo as if he called to me from across a wide gorge. Why didn't he tell me before now that my print meant nothing? Maybe he didn't have my fingerprint. If he did, maybe he was saving it for court.

"But before I get into the new info," he said, "I want to ask you something."

"Why don't you just tell me?" I groaned, unsure whether I'd tip over in the seat in a dizzy fit or whether I'd vomit on his radio.

"It can wait." Buhrman had developed an exquisite sense of interrogation timing.

He knows you're sick. Best time to trick you, make it stick.

"You still think it was an accident?" he said, a false note of incredulity in his voice belying his interrogation technique.

"Of course," I said. "There's no evidence otherwise, is there? No motive. Besides, I know my people. None of them are murderers."

"Well, Greer. Part of being a good boss is protecting your people. You do that?"

"Yeah. My workers are good people. I expect them to keep the law. The law's their final protection. This is America, Aaron. Everyone has rights. A whole Bill of Rights, in case you forgot. Did you forget that?" Buhrman's dogged hostility irritated me no matter how well-prepared for it I was.

"Hey, don't get mad. From what everybody tells me, your judgment's supposed to be pretty good. You seem like a straight enough guy to me. Been pretty helpful. So let's say I expected you to trust your people. I just want to know," he grit his teeth, "what about the one rotten apple that's all shiny and red, but under that skin, it's brown, turning black. Rotten to the core."

"It's possible. They'd have to be pretty smart, though. After a while, you work with somebody, you get to know them pretty well."

"Everybody's got something to hide. You can admit that." He caught himself in a statement and rephrased it. "Can you admit that?"

At that insinuation, I breathed deeply, pausing to let a wave of nausea decide whether it was staying or passing through. When it dwindled, I said, "It's not always that big a deal. Sometimes it's better to hide something."

Not bad, Chuck. Tell it true. Confuse this arrogant gumshoe.

Nausea tugged at my jaw again and something slipped up my throat. I had to slide down on the seat and the change in position shut me up.

"You sure you're all right?"

"Dizzy spell. Need some time off."

"Yeah, me too. This murder thing's a bitch. I never been so busy, mind never stops, paperwork, phone calls. I get why the smartest cop acts stupid, y'know. Old TV show—*Columbo*. You ever catch a re-run?"

He forgot I already called him a Columbo, but I just shook my head.

"No? Ya gotta see him in action. He's got so much going on upstairs he has to keep the info coming in at a speed he can manage. Sort, file it, move the pawns. That, and keeping criminals confused."

I was the last person in the world to sympathize with Buhrman's stress. Slumping, I stared at the a plastic replica of the town's emblem that was glued to the glove compartment, a blue hatchet crossed with a red plow on a field of triangular green pines. I supposed the town fathers wanted their descendants to remember who won the war between the savages and the farmers. The plow gleamed as if the Chief painted it with scarlet nail polish.

Chipper as the first morning of the universe, Burhman said, "Columbo's not like Monk. He's a normal guy, not some freak. He stopped talking and fiddled with his radio, reducing the volume on the static.

"One good thing..." he muttered.

I waited for him to finish his sentence. Then I caught on.

It's the old bait and switch. Maybe he has a snitch.

"Yeah?" I said. "Always a bright side to everything, eh, Aaron?" "That computer's becoming a friend of mine. Internet, downloading, email, Twister, MugBook. You must be into that stuff?"

"I got all the stuff. We're totally wired. You want to make money, you got no choice." My collegial attitude was starting to work.

Don't be a jerk. He's the one doing the work. On you.

"Charlie, I assume that anybody could have done this."

Watching him change direction like an angler dragging his lure across the current. "Anybody?"

"Yeah." He circled it closer.

"Not anybody," I said. "Even if it was murder, not everybody could do it. You ever meet a murderer?"

"Maybe. You never know. It's beside the point. In my line, you assume everybody can do it. Wouldn't you?"

I sat up and at that moment, the dizziness disappeared. Ready for a friendly argument, I said, "Maybe they can, just because they're human. As a human, you can say I can. As Charlie Greer, a specific human, I couldn't. Not only that, I wouldn't. How about you," I said, turning the tables again. "Can you kill someone?"

"Sure, if I had to. I'm trained to kill. I'm ready any time. It's not the favorite part of my job but if I had to uphold the law, stop somebody on a rampage? I'd do it. Decent people need protection. There's a lot of douche bag psychopath mental cases out there. What do you think they hired me for?"

I stared at him, shaking my head at the hypocritical twisted reasoning I'd come to expect from him.

"Don't look at me that way," Buhrman said. "Some asshole comes after you or your wife or kids? Don't tell me you wouldn't shoot him?"

"I don't own a gun."

"If you did, you would."

"Yeah, I would. No doubt. That's not murder. That's self-defense. It's legal. Society wants you to protect yourself and your family."

"What about the woman whose old man abused her for years before she finally shot him?"

"Sounds like self-defense."

"Jury disagreed. Second-degree murder. Gave her twenty years, said they'd thought about life, only it was second degree. I think the D.A. should have pushed all the way. She clearly premeditated it."

He switched on the siren and accelerated, passing a pick-up sagging with a load of firewood. As soon as he passed, he punched his steering wheel and the siren blurped into silence in mid-howl.

"What about that teenager in Florida? White guy shoots black kid. Self-defense?"

The Chief scowled.

Blue lights, speed, he's on a cops and robbers trip. Better bite your lip.

I deep-breathed a few times, showed him a poker face and said, "This discussion doesn't have anything to do with American Tofu, Aaron. Why don't you take me back to the factory?"

"You don't get it yet, do you, Greer?" he said as he swung the cruiser around in the middle of the street. "It looked like an accident, but it was too slick. Big woman. Strong. All the reports said you had good safety policies. Special training and all. You hadn't had an accident for what, 632 days straight? You posted the number for everyone to see."

"It's one of the best records in the food industry."

Ignoring my obvious pride in our safety record, Buhrman's zealotry twisted our competence into the realm of self-serving hypothetical mathematics.

"By my calculations, that makes a point zero zero one percent chance it was an accident. Those odds say we're on a one way street, my friend, straight down Homicide Lane."

He found a way to use my good business practices against me. Thank God I'd stayed in the saddle no matter how bad my body felt.

If I stayed home to heal my vertigo, Buhrman would snoop and claw around like some mutt with rabbit shit up his nose. He'd contrive some way to get at people and records and create so much fear that my employees would shiver when they saw him.

You stay home to satisfy your relaxation needs? Facts about you and Becky will sprout like weeds.

"I love statistics, Charlie. They reveal a lot of secrets. How about this one: nine out of ten of industrial accidents happen to men. So, repose that one and you get a one in ten chance Mac-Daniel should have an accident. See how it's addin' up to murder?"

His scatterbrained mathematics flummoxed me. He was so crazy maybe I should let him have free rein. Let everyone see him for his true Nazi persecutor self.

But, the fact was, everyone did have something to hide, including me, most of all, so I let my better judgment prevail. Nobody, nobody, never, ever needed to know anything about my harmless little affair with big strong Becky MacDaniel.

In his insistence on a conviction, Buhrman would weave a motive for Becky's death into his suspect's every ordinary, grubby deed and he'd have the support of the district attorney who didn't have an idea what Buhrman was up to. Lawyers be damned, I'd bust Buhrman as easily as he could bust me.

You ain't used to squirming. Why do it with Buhman?

I'd always been boss and whenever I wasn't top dog, I left the squabble. I couldn't leave this one, so I decided to take back as much control as I could. An image of Meng crossed my mind. How would he handle this conversation? Gambling that Buhrman didn't know a thing about my affair with Becky, I went on the offensive.

I sat up straight, my head cleared, my gut tightened. I felt buckled into the cruiser seat like a captain in a cockpit. I turned toward Buhrman and noticed how small he was. Narrow shoulders, thin thighs. He had to scoot the seat up as far forward as he could to reach the pedals.

"Yeah. We run a tight ship," I said. "Of course, you never know what can happen to your employees, on or off the job. Ask anyone in manufacturing, ask any employer. Do you follow up every accident at Pulzewski's Sausage Factory across town with a big investigation?"

He turned to me and slowed the car.

You're on a roll. Let yourself go.

My anger was coming on strong, sharpening my mind and tongue. I attacked. "Did you know the meat packing industry rips arms and heads off innocent people every day all across the country?" I paused, hoping it would sink in.

Buhrman dawdled along Main Street, listening, his chin jutting ahead under thin lips. The day's few pedestrians turned toward the cruiser, curious about the flashing lights.

I had the momentum. "A point zero zero one percent accident rate ought to win us an award from OSHA. It's so low, it's Guinness Book of Records. Go back and check your calculations before you make your conclusions about the street we're headed down."

He smirked.

"By the way," I said, with a calm, neutral tone, hoping he'd hear me without defenses and get the point right in his flat little gut. "Didn't I hear that the new deputy you hired for the night shift shot himself in the leg a few weeks ago? Was it an accident? Maybe somebody else shot him? Did you check his references before you hired him?"

Buhrman muttered, "This is not about the police, Greer."

"It might turn out to be, Aaron, if you don't get off this witch hunt. You still don't have any hard evidence, do you?" Now I had a chance to expose the one threat he could nab me with, the thing that was beyond my control, a possible fact. I asked, "What about that stuff under her fingernails. Did you get the DNA report?"

"Yeah."

I caught my breath. "Well?"

"Can't tell you."

"Christ, Aaron. I want to clear this up as much as you."

"Gotta save it for court, Charlie."

He's got nothing new. Back off, let him stew.

I let out my breath. The fake bait he flaunted in front of my face—"new information"—slipped right off his lure and the clever Charlie fish wiggled away, for now.

The "new information" I gave him about the meat industry and the accident in his own office should make him think before he waltzed onto my turf again as if he owned it.

Stay on course. Show him you can ride any bucking horse.

"One last question, Aaron," I said, maintaining the offensive. "You've never said why you think someone would kill Becky. Without a motive, you can't prove anybody's guilty, can you? With no motive, every lead or idea you have sends you on a wild goose chase. Basic logic, right?"

"Whad'ya mean?"

"Remember that first time you came to my office? You said you'd find a motive then you'd find the killer?"

"Charlie," he said, using my first name in a transparent effort to discount my points, "you're right. We don't tell the public we have The Motive. Why would we? You don't understand police work. Why do you think I have to investigate every angle? What you think is a wild goose chase is just solid old-time Beat the Bushes, Scare the Snakes. Do you know how much work that is?"

His narrow shoulders sagged and the beginnings of a wattle showed under his chin. The investigation had taken a lot out of him, too. Buhrman dropped me off at the factory and wished me a nice Thanksgiving. I watched him speed down the street with the cruiser's lights strobing violet shadows through the bare branches overhead. As he turned the corner, his siren wailed and retreated toward the center of town. I thought of the turkeys arriving at the chopping block suddenly understanding what their lives were all about.

***

I carved the turkey and ate Thanksgiving dinner with Nora and the kids, and went back to bed. By Saturday night, after seventy two hours of forgetting about my problems, I felt strong enough to go out for pizza and the movies with Chuck and Rissi.

Rissi and I sat down in our regular booth by the window at Jumbo's Pizza parlor while Chuckie climbed up on the bench behind me.

Rissi giggled. "Daddy, there's Chuckie."

I swung around and saw Chuckie's face mashed against the etched glass booth divider making a chimpanzee face at us. Rissi and I laughed together and Chuckie came and sat down beside his sister.

"My silly little monkeys," I said.

Rissi said, "Do monkeys cry, Daddy?"

"No, honey. Animals don't cry. Only people."

"Mommy says Chuckie's an animal and he cries."

Chuckie poked her in the shoulder. "No I'm not."

"You eat like one. Mommy says."

Chuckie stuck out his tongue and began licking Rissi's arm and neck and cheeks while she squealed and pushed him away. After they settled down to wait for our plain cheese pizza, Rissi studied me with her frank six-year-old's stare, then she said, "Daddy, did you have a fight?"

"Why, honey?"

"You have two black eyes."

I hadn't realized that the bags under my eyes were so dark. *Little kids see the facts. You can't fool your girl with your public acts.*

I'd been slugging it out, now taking a break between rounds thirteen and fourteen of a battle that would go on till the last man standing.

With the comforting odors of sizzling cheese and sweet dough baking, my seven year-old son traced a maze in the chili pepper flakes he'd poured on the tabletop, listening to us while his eyes focused on the peppers. I appreciated the sweetest lovingest little girl in the world who worried about her old papa, and my heart creaked. Tears leaked from my eyes.

"What's the matter, Daddy? Why you crying? Do your eyes hurt?" she asked. Chuck snapped his head up from his pepper play and frowned when he saw me crying and smiling at the same time. "No fights, honey," I said. "Daddy's been working way too hard." "Why you crying then?"

"There's happy crying. You know happy crying? I'm so happy to be sitting here waiting to eat the best pizza in New York with the two most beautiful smartest kids I love more than anything in the whole world."

"When Mommy cries, she's sad. I guess it's different for girls and boys."

She's wise. No surprise.

I laughed and sniffled, wiping my eyes with a napkin. "You said it, Rissi. It's different for girls and boys."

She changed her tone and aimed a disapproving, purse-lipped stare at her brother. "Daddy, if Chuck licks his fingers now, he'll burn his tongue. Mommy always tells him to leave the peppers alone."

Chuck immediately stabbed his fingers between his lips and shoved his face up to his sister's, twisting his hand around the inside of his mouth as if he was unscrewing a bottle cap. In two seconds, his eyes bulged, he coughed and gagged and panted. He poured his Seven-Up into his mouth and over his lips and chin, splashing his shirt and the table, then he grabbed my water and sloshed it down. "Chuckie," I said, laughing, "go to the bathroom and wash your mouth out with cold water until it stops burning."

"It's her fault," he said. "Don't laugh at me." Big tears flowed off his cheeks. Rissi and I raised our eyebrows at each other and shrugged our shoulders as he dashed off to the bathroom.

My son, I thought. My beautiful son and daughter.

Protect their innocence. It's the only way you can make a difference.

That night, after packing the kids off to bed, Nora and I stayed up late in bed, reading, but we never opened the massage manual. She practiced some acupressure on my forearms, to dispel the stale chi that was stuck in my body, she said.

"When you get dizzy, it's old chi trying to move. Somehow it gets stuck in your head, like some dam's in there holding it back." At least she must have been reading the massage book.

"I watched a video about this. When you move, old chi wobbles like a big pot of soup and makes you dizzy."

I thought her diagnosis was as good as any. She squeezed and pressed a couple of sensitive spots and then said, "Can we talk?"

Nora and I had avoided serious conversations outside of therapy and I was actually sick of talking about what's for dinner, what did the kids do in school, how're sales, did we hire any new workers. Now that I'd let my Shu Ling fantasies go, maybe I could open up to Nora for serious talk, if that's what she wanted.

"Sure but, remember, we agreed we won't get heavy just before we fall asleep." I reached out and put my arm around her, pulling her toward me. She lay her cheek on my chest.

"Sometimes you suspend the rules," she said.

"Yeah. We gotta get this investigation wrapped up. If it went away, we'd be fine."

"Would we? Is that all it is, Charlie, the investigation?"

"That and work. Soy to the World is the biggest marketing project I've ever tried. It could change the face of the industry."

"I know, I know. But I'm worried about you, honey."

"Oh, thank you, baby. I'm all right. Little tired is all."

"I'm more worried about us."

The relationship. To a woman, everything else is just a blip.

"That's why we're in therapy, sweetie. Working things out." "We're not making much progress. I don't think you're really present in therapy, any more than you are at home."

She was right. I opened myself up as little as I could get away with but I said, "What do you mean? I haven't missed one session." "You sit there like a lump of dough."

"C'mon. We have great talks."

"You talk. You can always talk. I don't know what you feel. I can't tell any more." Nora pulled away and stretched out on her back. "I'm so sad when we're together."

I turned on to my side and propped myself up on my elbow. "Sweetie, I don't know. I've been out of it. Give us some time. We can get through this. Think of the kids."

"I think of myself, the kids, you. I think of everything, Charlie. I always have and you barely think about anything except your work."

I noticed I was clenching my jaws and breathing quicker. The last thing I wanted was a fight on the first night I'd been relaxed in weeks. I lay down on my back and said, "Can't we do this in therapy? I'm sorry, honey. I've been a lousy husband."

"You didn't used to be."

"There's hope, then, right?"

"I don't know, Charlie. We've fallen so far apart, we'll be lucky to make it back."

"Hey, that's enough. We've still got two months of Year of the Monkey luck."

"Some luck."

"Luck's not something you know you have while you're having it, Nora. You see it when you review your life later."

"Oh, Charlie. I'm too tired to listen to your pontifications." She snapped off her bedside light and rolled onto her side, facing away from me.

With my hand on her back, I said, "Let's go away, after the New Year. How about Spain or someplace warm but not too hot?"

"We can talk about it later."

You can still make it, even if you have to fake it. You know you should. It'll feel good.

I scooted over to her and spooned my body into hers. We fit perfectly. I cupped her breast in my hand and moved my pelvis against her bottom, wondering if she would respond. She swiveled her neck and kissed me on the lips, then turned back and sighed, falling asleep in about ten seconds.

That night, I slept without waking up once. That was it for my dizzy spells, except for one last small one the next afternoon. I think it came from eating too much whipped cream on the last three pieces of Nora's left-over pumpkin pie.

Chapter Twelve

Genevieve

WHERE'S LIAM?

Wegmans Markets in Rochester had always been my best customer. As I learned from Gianni, Wegmans "...owns Rochester." When I told that to a seatmate on a plane once, he replied, "I thought Kodak owned Rochester." We laughed and agreed that between the two companies, Rochester was thoroughly owned by some powerful masters and Kodak was great in its day, but now it's history. Wegmans will always be around.

The most relaxing part of my job was giving tofu cooking demonstrations in supermarkets. I put on a good show because I wanted the store managers to value me as entertainment for their customers. Modern food store marketing assumes that people hate having to shop because no one has time to prepare food any more. So if you showed them a good time while they did their chores, they'd feel better and spend more money. When I put on a lively demo, I built my reputation as a top performer with the corporate office and it didn't matter to them what I was touting as long as it sold.

I staged my best demos in the Wegmans stores. I'd arrive on a Saturday morning, load a cart with pots, an electric wok, a toaster oven, and roll it into a bright spot in the produce aisle somewhere between the potatoes and the bean sprouts. I'd prop up my easel and sign, and start chopping tofu and vegetables. No matter what recipe I demo-ed, I sautéed clove after clove of garlic, so its aroma would waft over the whole store, advertising my demo, enticing the hungry as well as the curious, all with shopping dollars lurking in their purses waiting to leap out. My bait wasn't tofu, but the exotic.

My message to the shoppers was. 'I'm just like you. I can chop and stir and talk and smile, all at once, like any mother, like everyworking woman anywhere." I wasn't acting—maybe just a little to keep the show entertaining—and the shoppers respected me for showing up with the real Gen. That made demoing a pleasure. Usually.

At the beginning of my tofu demos career, I'd compose recipes like "Tofu Dengaku" or "Gohiji Dofu." The novelty appealed to people but too many sampled without buying. The authentic Chinese and Japanese recipe names sounded strange and impossible to prepare.

At one demo, a produce manager, flirting with me, asked me if I could fix him scrambled eggs and fried potatoes, to "bring out the men."

So I did, except I made scrambled tofu with turmeric added to give it an eggy color. He couldn't tell the difference between scrambled eggs and the crumbled, yellow tofu. He wolfed it down. When I told him he'd just eaten half a pound of tofu and reduced the cholesterol in his blood by 50%, he laughed and promised he'd never let me trick him again. I noticed that he stuck a recipe brochure into his pocket.

After that, I created and demoed recipes any American could recognize. Charlie loved my marketing slogan: 'Tofu the American Way.'

"Why didn't I think of that?" he said. "It's so obvious. Gen the Genius strikes again."

Sometimes I didn't know if Charlie praised me or mocked me so I let it slide. He painted the company trucks with the phrase and we used it in all of our sales literature.

***

Since Becky's death in the factory, I'd been so busy that Liam and I had less time than usual together. When I asked him if he'd like to do a demo with me in Wegmans Superstore in Buffalo, he said, "Sure, Mom. I bet I sell more tofu than you."

He and I made an irresistible sales act: Working Mom and Charming Son. I taught Liam that, as long as we told the truth, we could sell anything. We proved it. As we handed out samples, I'd say things like, "Yeah. We work Saturdays so we can be together." Which was true. Then Liam would offer someone a taste of tofu, chiming in with, "Gotta save up for college." That was true, too.

I didn't tell him that just because he was with me, people would buy two packages of tofu rather than one.

Between bursts of customers, Liam roamed around the store, chatting with managers and stock clerks usually ending up hanging around the in-store bakery. The bakers in the Buffalo store insisted that he gorge on cream horns and sticky buns as a reward for helping me and for having to eat so much tofu. I let him eat as many as he wanted.

Three weeks before Christmas, we put on our last supermarket demo of the year. I'd contrived a cranberry tofu Christmas dessert that sold ten cases of tofu before lunch. Liam left our little stand just before noon to visit the bakery for a special lunch treat. He'd had a swim meet the night before and felt a little tired, so I told him to take an hour off. By one o'clock, I was serving Working Woman's Quick Casserole to a flood of customers, so I couldn't shut down the demo to find him. When the crowd thinned, it was already one-thirty and I wondered where he was. I unplugged my pans and covered my cart then hurried to the bakery.

He wasn't there. They'd given him two bear claws around noon, and he'd taken them and gone. I circled the store, checking every aisle, visiting every kiosk. No one had seen him and I asked all the clerks and shelf-stockers to watch for him. Fear began to claw at my chest.

I burst into the walk-in cooler, calling "Liam. Liam. Are you in here? Come out."

The absolute hush of cheese wheels and milk crates and beef haunches answered me. Breathlessly, I raced through the back room, slamming open the freezer door, fearing I'd find him locked in, stiff and lifeless on the floor. Thank God, it was only boxes of microwave dinners and ice cream perched on shelves in dim light.

I ran to the customer service desk and asked them to page him to the tofu demo. I raced up and down every aisle, bumping into the backs and butts of foraging shoppers, tripping over their carts.

I asked everybody "Have you seen a 12-year old black-haired boy wearing a red sweatshirt?"

They all gawked at me with wide eyes.

"No."

"Sorry."

"Sorry."

"No."

"We'll watch for him."

"I thought I saw a kid in a red sweatshirt. Back at the meat counter."

"Yeah. At the bakery."

"Maybe he's at produce?"

"Did you check the parking lot?"

"You'll find him. My grandson always wanders off."

"Wish I could help."

"Good luck."

The supermarket pager called his name over and over into the emptiness. My heart raced and I sprinted back to the demo to wait for him.

A knot of women clustered around my table, expecting me to begin cooking.

"I'm sorry. I can't demo right now. My son disappeared. Have you seen a black-haired boy wearing a red Bills sweatshirt?"

Most of them were mothers and they said they'd help. The sympathy in their eyes made me feel more scared, but I showed them the picture of Liam that I carried in my wallet, then they fanned out across the store. Two women volunteered to scout the parking lot and another said she'd check around the recycling bins. "They're always full of things boys like to investigate," she said, stroking my arm.

By two o'clock I was in the store manager's office, on the phone to the police. I called Charlie at home, leaving a message on his machine that I'd stopped the demo because Liam had taken off and I couldn't find him. I asked him or Nora to call me as soon as they got the message. The police showed up in ten minutes, but the pity on their faces tore my heart out.

I started having trouble breathing. Burning air caught in my throat, gagging me. I willed my chest to relax while all around me, people faded into a fog and sounds dulled to a grating wind that cut through my body, chilling me. I don't know how long that lasted, but eventually, my chest began to loosen up and heave and tears gushed from my eyes. Trying to speak, all I could do was cough and grunt.

A big, motherly woman sergeant-in-charge sat beside me, pulling me into her soft shoulder with one arm, pushing my hair off my forehead and dabbing my cheeks with a Kleenex.

"Don't worry, Genny," she said, rocking me in her arms. "We'll find him, honey. We have plenty of time. Probably wandering around the neighborhood. You know boys, always curious."

Her warm voice comforted me enough that I emerged from near total numbness.

"I'm Darlene," she said. "Got kids of my own. My Bobbie, when he was twelve? Vanished on us one afternoon in the State Park. Gave us the shock of our life." She squeezed my arm. "He came back. Thought he saw some deer. Wanted to get closer. Time he noticed where he was, it was twilight. That's when we panicked. All of a sudden, he comes strollin' up the hill from the lake like a ghost."

I barely heard her.

"When he got closer, he laughed at us. At first, I wanted to slap him silly. Then we hugged and hugged, and cried and cried. We ended up stayin' till the Park closed, burnin' marshmallows and fillin' our faces with S'mores like we'd never tasted anything so fine."

I smiled weakly but she interested me only for as long as she was telling me her story. I was glad she found him, but I'd heard too many stories about kids who never came back. I pushed her away.

"I'm fine. Can't we get to work finding my son?"

For what seemed like hours, she and her staff interviewed me, customers, store managers, clerks. They asked if we'd seen any suspicious characters, if we had any relatives in Buffalo, whether Liam often went off by himself.

"Of course he does. He's a boy."

Their list seemed endless and I had no idea how it would help. Right now he was in danger and all their questions did was stall. They persisted: Was he a curious kid or did he stay close to home? Was he into music? What kind of rules did I have about his not taking rides from strangers? When they asked the manager did the store have any security discs we could review? I got excited. He went to check and came back in five minutes carrying three tapes.

He shoved the first one into the DVD player. It flickered on. An overview of the whole store, it showed an empty produce aisle. I read the digital clock in the lower right of the screen. "04.27.29."

"That's this morning," I said. "The middle of the night."

Embarrassed, he ejected the tape and inserted the next.

Same view, different time. "05.33.47." We watched it turn to "05:44.00" before he ejected it.

"This should be it," he said. "Unless they fucked up again. 'Scuse my language."

"Just play it," I said.

Same view. "06:53.21."

"Shit," he said. He turned to me and Darlene, his face red and scrunched up like he was about to cry. He grabbed the phone and started hollering into it. Everyone else in the office started talking at once. Standing around and talking.

Finally, I screamed. "God damn it! Do something! Don't just stand there blabbering! It's my son's life!"

They tried to calm me, offering me a Valium and Darlene tried to hug me again, but I shrugged her off. The store manager slipped a cup into my hand. "Drink this," he said. "It'll help."

I sniffed the liquid—straight bourbon. I narrowed my eyes at him, letting him know what I thought of his competence as a store manager, and I gulped the whiskey down.

I'd never felt more helpless in my life. Nora wasn't home, no way would I call Liam's Dad. Robert would terrorize me for the rest of my life about this. I wished I could call Gianni. He'd understand but what could he do? I almost called Benko because I just needed somebody, anybody I knew, to be with me. In that helpless afternoon, I realized how all-by-myself I was in life. I knew hundreds of people, had dozens of friends I would do anything for whenever they asked. But in reality, I had nobody but Liam, and nobody who cared about him the way I do.

Liam's disappearance galvanized everyone in the store into some kind of action. A grocery bagger came up with the idea of making blow-up copies of my wallet photo of Liam and posting them around the neighborhood.

One of the women who'd come to the store just to attend my demo offered to call her son-in-law who worked at a local TV station. She wanted to fax him the photo and have him run it on the news. That was one of the best ideas I'd heard. She left with a photo of Liam cradled in her hands, his beautiful smile glittering with silver braces, his eyes shining with mischief.

I couldn't sit still. Darlene stayed beside me wherever I went, circling the parking lot ten times, peering into every car, handing out copies of the photo with my and Darlene's cell phone numbers written on the back.

I jerked apart every column of grocery carts littering the lot. Darlene had the warehouse clerk call up the trucking companies that had unloaded earlier, but since it was Saturday, only three trucks had stopped by the store. All of them were gone before Liam and I had arrived.

My mind boiled with images of Liam laying twisted in a ditch, filthy water flowing over his head. I saw him chained in the back of a dented, rusty van, surrounded by brutes prodding him with knives. I saw his picture on a milk carton on the kitchen table in his friend's house where he should have been having breakfast after a sleep-over. I saw his empty grave in our family cemetery on the Connecticut coast, right next to my mother's tombstone…

I began to offer God anything He wanted if only He'd bring Liam back. I'd spend every weekend at homeless shelters…I'd adopt a meth baby…I'd teach cooking classes at the Senior Center…I'd have sex only if I was engaged to somebody…

"God," I bargained, "give me this one little miracle and you can have me for the rest of my life."

The police organized some store employees into a search team that went out into the neighborhood, knocking on doors, pinning Liam's face up on all the telephone poles. An ambulance sat quietly parked next to a fire truck near the front entrance to the store. Police cruisers roamed back and forth regularly in front of the store.

A crowd of catastrophe vampires had gathered nearby. Every now and then, one would shout something encouraging like "Hang in there. He'll come back." Then a woman bellowed at me: "Kids run away from mothers who beat them."

When I heard that I tore loose from Darlene. I would have killed the woman if one of the policemen hadn't held me while another escorted her to her car and guided her out the exit.

About the time the lights came on over the parking lot, my lungs seized up again as the dusk settled around me like a shroud. If Liam didn't come back before nightfall, I was afraid I'd never see him again. I leaned against Darlene as she escorted me to the ambulance where the EMT's laid me down and put an oxygen mask over my face.

Within a minute, my head cleared and my terror ebbed. I sat up and tore the mask off. I stepped out of the ambulance's rear door just as Liam emerged from between some parked cars and headed for the supermarket's front door.

I screamed "Liam!" and flew across the sidewalk. He glanced around, then spotted me and gave me a big smile. The crowd parted for me as I rushed to him and grabbed him, hugging him, picking him up and pressing him into my body as if I wanted to stuff him back inside where he'd be safe. The crowd burst into applause.

I felt Liam's heart beating fast against my chest, his quick breaths chafing my ears like brushes. I heard the clapping from each pair of hands, the pounding steps on the asphalt of police and the employees as they ran to watch us. The parking lot lights cast a moist yellow halo around Liam's head.

"Oh, sweetie. God. You're safe. God. Thank you." I blubbered and grinned and cried. Sounds of sobbing rose from the crowd.

Liam pushed back against my hands. "Mom, what's going on?" He stared at the police and the EMTs. "Why are all these people here?" Attracted by the blinking red lights of the emergency vehicles, he tried to turn around to see through the surrounding mob.

I gripped Liam's shoulders as hard as I could, holding him tightly, but pushing him back to arm's length. "Where have you been, young man?" I said, still breathless.

"You know. Niagara Falls."

"Niagara Falls!"

The words "Niagara Falls" rippled through the crowd.

"Niagara Falls! How did you get there?"

"I'm sorry, Mom. I thought it'd be okay."

With him in my arms, my fears washed away. Anger began to rise into my face. "How did you get there, young man?"

"Benko. You know."

"Benko?"

The word "Benko" echoed out of the crowd.

"He's your friend, too, Mom."

All I could say was "Benko?"

"We went and came back as fast as we could. I'd never seen it from Canada before. You always said it's good to try new things. It was beautiful. All ice castles and stuff."

I shouted for the policewoman. "Where is he? That asshole. He can't do this to me! Darlene, find the man who kidnapped him." "Where is this Benko, son?" Darlene asked Liam.

"I don't know. He let me off in the parking lot."

Darlene put her muscular arms around both of us, pushing us gently into the store while the police dispersed the crowd of shoppers. She signaled to one of the EMTs to follow us. In the store manager's office, Liam sat shirtless on the manager's desk while the EMT examined him for marks.

"I'm fine, Mom. Don't make such a fuss. I was having a good time."

"You were having a good time?" I shouted. "What kind of time do you think I was having? I was afraid somebody kidnapped you. I thought I'd never see you again." Now that he was back, I released the hysteria I'd bottled up since I noticed he was gone.

"Mom, take it easy. I'm back. I'm all right."

I refused to let him console me. "You're in big trouble, young man. The whole city of Buffalo was on alert for you."

"Didn't you get my note?" Liam asked.

"What note?" I said, a shudder streaking up my back.

"The one I left in the bakery with the cookie lady."

Having listened to us intently, the store manager immediately called down to his bakery supervisor. Liam's sniffles made the only sound in the room while we all waited for the supervisor to find the note. In a minute, the manager, still on the phone, nodded to me, grinning like an idiot. His job was saved. He told the employee to bring the note to his office.

"I'd never split without telling you," Liam said, tears flowing again.

"I know, honey," I said, hugging him. I felt relieved and confused. I blamed myself for not being careful, for mistrusting Liam. "That's why I was so worried."

The bakery supervisor entered the office, handing the note to her boss. She said, "It was laying under some wax paper. I'm surprised we even saw it." He read it and, with a sour face, passed it to me.

Mom I'm going to Canada with Benko to see Niagara Falls It's gonna be LOUD
Back later to help You pack up
Your son Liam
P.S. You win the selling contest!!!!

"I gave it to somebody standing there. I asked him to give it to Nancy. He said he would. I'm sorry, Mom. I didn't want to get you upset."

The manager threw his hands up and announced to the ceiling, "She's fired. They're fired. What a mess."

"No, don't fire them. It's not their fault," I said.

"It's nobody's fault," Liam said.

"No. It's somebody's fault." I seethed. "Benko had no right to take you without speaking to me."

"Do you want us to arrest this Benko?" Darlene asked. "You can charge him with any number of things. Up to kidnapping. Could be Federal. Going into Canada, doesn't matter he brought the boy back. Least you can do is scare the devil outta him."

"I'm tempted. I want to. I don't know." I thought for a minute. "Do I have to make up my mind right now?"

"Give yourself some time to calm down. We got twenty-four hours at least, maybe longer, 'less he runs. Lemme know tomorrow. If I were you, I'd give this Benko somethin' serious to think about," she counseled. "It's up to you. Was me? I'd have him in jail in five minutes."

"It's not that easy. I can't think straight. Maybe it was innocent. He was my old boyfriend."

"Did you dump him?"

I nodded my head yes.

"Worst kind. You better take care of this," Darlene said. "Your son could be in real trouble."

I had to find out what was going on. Liam liked Benko and lately, Benko had been calm and friendly on the phone. The night before when I told him we were going to Buffalo, he did ask what store we'd be at, but if I threw him in jail, what would happen when he got out?

In another hour, strength returned to my adrenaline-drained muscles. Liam and the bakery crew packed up our demo, telling me it was the least they could do. I thanked everyone.

"We're happy everything turned out all right," the manager said. His voice was pinched, holding back anger, and I expected I'd hear from the Wegmans front office before long. No doubt the manager was calculating how much money this distraction had cost the company and how much it had reduced his bonus. I was sure I had a good enough reputation with everyone in the store as well as the company headquarters to withstand their dissatisfaction. Besides, if anybody asked, I'd tell them what fast, caring response they'd given to a mother in distress. Publicity like that was priceless, so I wasn't worried about the manager.

I doubted they'd have much more to say to me than "Be careful" and send out a memo to all food demonstrators: "Leave your children home!" Charlie would hear from them, for sure. That was the last thing I cared about.

***

That night I sent Liam to bed as soon as we got home. He protested that he didn't deserve a punishment. It wasn't his fault that the man in the bakery forgot to give Nancy his note. "I always wanted to do something with Benko so I figured this was a good time. I'm sorry I left you all the demo work."

"It has nothing to do with the work, Liam."

"Benko said we'd see the purest water in the world. You always said American Tofu was made from the purest water."

"Liam!"

"I would've come and told you but you were too busy—you had a hundred ladies crowding around your table. I couldn't get through. Benko said a note would be good enough. You should see those ice palaces and caves. Everyone says this is the best time of year—"

"What? He told you not to tell me in person?"

"I tried," he moaned.

"You didn't try hard enough. Besides, who does Benko think he is, telling my son how to behave with his mother? Not even your father can make up rules for you when you're with me. You know that."

"Mom, I'm growing up. I can do a lot of stuff on my own."

"You're not that old that you can go running off in the middle of a strange city and leave me alone wondering where the hell you are!" I spun around and left before I lost my temper completely. "You're grounded until further notice."

Leaving Liam sobbing in his room, I immediately called Benko. "Yes?"

"How dare you take my son without telling me! You can't do that! I could have you arrested. They'll deport you back to Russia where you belong!"

"Genevieve. Wait."

"Who do you think you are? You can't just take him someplace because you want to! I could charge you with kidnapping! The police are on my side. They want to pick you up right now. You'd be in jail in ten minutes if I wanted it. I could have you deported!" The phone was silent. "Benko! Do you hear me?"

"Don't bring cops into this, Genevieve. Real bad if you did."

"Bad? For who? For you! Liam is my son."

"Genevieve, a minute. Wait. He's all right?"

I fumed, not answering.

"Answer me."

"He's okay."

"He had good time. Yes?"

I admitted that, too.

"So, what's your problem?"

"You didn't get my permission. You can't do that. This is America. We respect mothers here! You abducted him!"

"Need your permission? You're so busy, I figure, help her out.

Take kid for a few minutes. Give him good time. She'll like me better."

"Like you better? I almost had a heart attack."

"Can I take Liam anywhere I want? Sure, you know. With me he'll go, anytime. For a father, he's starved in his life. Like you, for a man, you're starved. But smart, Liam he's real smart boy. Not like mother." His voice seethed with bitterness.

"Shut up! Listen to me. I can call the police and they'll have you behind bars before you can hide your vodka."

"Don't. You'll be too sorry."

"Just leave us alone."

"I'm giving you a present—break from every minute child care, that's all."

"That's nice, Benko. If it's true, you have to talk to me about that."

"Sorry you're upset. Right now I come over. Make you feel good."

"I'm in no mood. I'm still thinking about calling the cops."

He gentled his tone, his words almost purring in his rumbling register. "How do you think I feel? You don't want anymore to see me? Little police chief scared you? He's prick. Tiny cock. No balls."

His voice deepened further, growling with menace. "You know, Disney World? He'd like to go, Liam said. Good plan, taking him. Let's go to Florida, Gen."

An icicle fell from my throat into my stomach. My jaw went numb.

"Gen?"

Had Benko purposely taken Liam to get revenge on me for dumping him? He just told me he'd steal Liam again if I didn't change my attitude toward him.

I imagined Benko drunk in a chair with a fire raging around him, licking at his clothes and hair as he lay unconscious, burning him out of my life. Then, I saw him lying lifeless, crushed under a big machine in the factory. I shivered.

"Genevieve, are you here? You need little hug." He purred. "It's been long day. After demos, I know how tired you get. I remember after one demo you had me come over for long nice foot rub. What about tonight? Nice rub, start with feet then all over?"

I tried to figure out what to do. I could have him arrested. Then, as soon as he was released, I'd suffer his fury and I had no way to predict how bad that would be. I could get a restraining order but that would was enrage him. Benko would probably come after me just to prove I couldn't control him, even with the law on my side.

I was afraid. Still, I had to veil my anger until I could make sure Liam and I were safe. "Benko, you know I didn't drop you. I had no choice. It's for your own good as much as mine. That Chief snoops everywhere. Once this blows over, well...A foot rub would be nice," I said, trying to cajole him, "but I'm totally wiped out tonight."

"Ah, Genevieve. Gentle little rub. Nothing else? I bring you to life. Your skin wants my 'silky' touching?"

"Benko, I'm out of it." I inhaled. With as much friendship in my voice as I could muster, I said, "Do me one favor. That's all. Until they close the case on the MacDaniel woman, please, stick to our agreement. We can't see or talk to each other."

"What about work? I'm nicer to you at work now, right?"

"Yes. At work. In public. But don't come around Liam."

"If you say so, beautiful woman. You know, Liam comes to me, what can I do?"

"He won't."

"You don't know. He's growing up. Twelve? What they want, boys start to do what they want—not what mother wants. Disney World he talks about. I like Florida, too. Warm. Sunny. Nice place for kids."

"Benko, shut up. Good night."

"Genevieve, I'm sorry you got so upset. Take it easy. For your health it's way bad."

He laughed. I ended the call, my hands shaking. The adrenaline seeped out of my muscles and I collapsed again, weeping, my arms and legs trembling. He hadn't really threatened me or Liam directly, but I felt us in danger.

Maybe I was just so exhausted that I didn't understand him. Did he take Liam to Niagara Falls because Liam asked him to? Maybe the offer of a foot rub was genuine. I didn't want to make him my enemy but I couldn't trust him now. My mind was totally befuddled and half-paralyzed with fear. I had to get out, or I'd go mad. Or worse, I'd hurt somebody, somebody named Benko.

I'd just survived the most harrowing day of my life. I flopped down on the couch, waiting to sink into the soothing arms of sleep. But Benko's gravelly voice saying "...boys do what they want" and "I like Florida, too" echoed through my brain until finally, not even my fears for Liam could keep me awake.

***

Sun pouring through my window sent me into a dream of sweating in the desert and woke me out of a deep sleep. An English muffin spread with my favorite strawberry jam and a steaming cup of Irish Breakfast tea sat on the coffee table next to me. Liam sat in the rocker, the comics in his lap. Love for him bloomed in my chest and throat, sprouting petals of tears from my eyes.

He glanced up and sprung off his chair. Wrapping his arms around my neck, he said, "Don't cry, mom. I'm sorry. Next time, I'll tell you in person. I promise."

We hugged and I stopped crying. I pushed my rag of a body to sitting position and offered him a bite of the muffin. He'd laid the strawberry jam on an inch thick, something I'd never do, but I relished Liam's caring. We read the comics together on the couch and I asked him about Niagara Falls. He didn't want to say much, but when I encouraged him, he became so excited, I promised to take him back in the spring.

"Can we take the boat under the falls?"

"If it's not too cold," I said. "But Liam, promise me one thing?"

"What?"

"Don't ever go with Benko or anybody else again."

"What if I ask you first? I have to go places with somebody," he said with all the logic he could muster. "You're not around all the time."

"That's true," I said. "But for now, until I get over what happened, ask me way ahead of time. Do you understand?"

"Sure, mom. Will you tell me when you're over it?" he said, squeezing my hand.

I heard my own optimism and persuasiveness in his voice. He'd learned well. Right then, I wished I'd taught him to be a little more afraid of the world.

Chapter Thirteen

Genevieve

CONFESSION IN THE KITCHEN

It's impossible for a mother to know just how much damage a child can inflict on himself and still be normal. If he gets hurt, should she blame him, bad luck, or herself?

Every few months, Liam hurt himself badly enough to go to the emergency room. He bruised his shin at soccer so deeply that he had to wear a plastic cast. Then he launched himself over his handlebars while he was biking in the woods, landing on his shoulder and head. Thank God he'd paid attention to me and worn his helmet. He sported the six stitches in his chin like a combat medal.

Then, the week after the Wegmans incident, when Liam sprained his wrist playing volleyball at gym in school and the school sent him to the ER for treatment, Ron Michelson, the emergency room doctor called me asked me to come in for a talk about Liam.

He was one of the Clementines who'd asked me out. He was too short for me, and every doctor I'd ever gone out with jumped me almost before they said hello, so I told him I was involved with someone from out of town. I thought I'd let him down gently but after the interview about Liam, I wasn't sure.

"I just wondered if there was anything wrong at home?"

"Nothing unusual, Ron," I said, taken aback.

"I asked only because when a kid shows a pattern of accidents, sometimes he's acting out emotional troubles. If there's something going on, and we can help…Well, you know, we're here to help."

The last thing I needed was the medical authorities prying into our life. I started to smolder. "You think he has a pattern?" He may have been well-meaning and I didn't want to appear guilty by reason of defensiveness.

"Well, we do see him a lot."

"What do you expect? He's a lively kid. He thinks he can do anything."

"Maybe you should slow down. He's probably just modeling you. How have you been feeling?"

I really didn't like him telling me what to do, but I thought he might have a point about Liam. He needed me to be home with him. "You know, I've been a single mother for twelve years now. Maybe Liam has grown up faster than other kids his age. He's still a new kid in town. Bound to show off sometimes, take it over the top."

"I just had to ask," he said, taking my hand. "I want to make sure you're doing well, too."

I hoped he wasn't planning to ask me out again. I didn't want to reject him, but I resented a sneaky power play.

"You know one of our workers died in the factory?" I said. "Who doesn't?"

"That's put a lot of strain on me," I said, withdrawing the hand, but smiling, encouraging him to continue his mock-compassionate tone.

He nodded sympathetically. "I bet."

"Liam's probably feeling some of that," I said, intending to assuage his concern about my flakiness with a gentle reminder that I was in the middle of a crisis.

"That could do it," Ron said. He urged me to take some time off and to relax with Liam.

I worried that Ron may have had a point about Liam's accidents. Just because he wanted to go out with me didn't mean I should ignore warning signs, especially since I could be responsible. After Wegmans and my constant distraction with Benko and the fact that I'd begun to lean on Gianni to get me a new job, I didn't doubt that Liam had picked up my worries. I hoped Liam hadn't created a pattern of hurting himself to bring my attention back to him.

Before I left the interview with Ron, his caring questions convinced me that Liam might have a problem.

I met with Liam's counselor at school, told her my fears, and asked her to try to find out whether my son had any issues I didn't know about—with his friends, teachers, any weird thing that could happen to a beautiful child who might be afraid to reveal it to his mother. After she and Liam talked several times, she reported that, as far as she could tell, Liam was just a rambunctious kid.

She had to hug me for five minutes while I sobbed my relief into her shoulder. Surprised by the depth of my anxiety under the tears, I decided to take Ron's advice and go on a real vacation over the Christmas holidays when Liam would go to Robert in Boston.

***

Despite a week of vegging-out, long slow swims at the club, and silence at home, with no stimulation other than my daily phone calls with Liam, Christmas vacation ended with me tired, not in the best shape to start a six-week Chinese New Year push of sales. The low skies and sub-freezing temperatures made me want to get on the first plane to Miami.

Then the one warm star in my life came home from spending his Christmas vacation with Robert. Liam limped into the house with a broken toe.

"Me'n Dad were swimming at the Y. Dad tossed me up and I came down a little crooked. Banged my foot against the side of the pool.

"It's nothing, Mom," he said. "The doctor says I'll be running on it in a few weeks. Relax. It wasn't Dad's fault. I was trying a flip."

I couldn't help worrying, no matter what the counselor said about his high energy level. What next?

That night over dinner, Liam asked me why I was upset.

I said, "No reason, honey."

"Mom, you always bite your lips and hunch your shoulders when you're worried. Tell me. I can take it. We're friends, remember?"

Liam's reading of my feelings brought tears to my eyes. "I have a lot on my mind right now. The next month or so we won't be seeing each other so much and I don't like that."

"We'll talk. I'll be fine."

He meant to assure me but I didn't like pressuring Liam with my melancholy, even though the most important teaching I could ever give him was emotional honesty.

"I know, honey. I'm just glad you're home safe with me again." "You'll still come to the regional swim meet, right?"

"Nothing would keep me away. I told Charlie I have priorities."

Liam reached over and caressed my cheek. As we started to eat, tears dripped off my chin into my tortellini. He handed me his napkin. "Take this for your nose. You're gonna make your pasta all slimy."

He made me laugh deeper than anybody in the world.

***

Liam, me, Charlie, Nora, a lot of the workers who'd had accidents on the job, Charlie's kids who'd been sick off and on for two months—all of us were victims of some toxic cloud of grief and doubt raining misery on us since Becky died. It poured on Charlie and splattered off his broad back onto the rest of us. Our record days without an accident was ancient history.

Charlie's distress fueled his determination to make a huge recovery from our poor sales in the fall. Out of guilt about my upcoming departure from American Tofu and loyalty to Nora and Charlie, I let Charlie pile on more work than anyone in her right mind could handle. For our Year of the Rooster tofu promotion, he arranged a seven-city media tour for me with eight TV and six radio shows and who knows how many newspaper interviews, all crammed between January nineteenth and twenty-ninth.

With his inflated plans, Charlie settled the future of the company on my shoulders. A few months ago, I might have welcomed it, but now, my to-do list hung over me like a tipping boulder about to fall.

I couldn't believe it once I wrote down everything I had to do. Sixty-five supermarket sales phone calls, five dozen demos to schedule, 2000 posters to design, photograph, print, distribute, not to mention all the TV and radio shows to prepare for, and the hotel reservations. How was I going to find good hotels in cities I'd never been in? Plus, I had to make arrangements for Liam while I was gone, not to mention the blog and Facebook.

I knocked on Charlie's office door and without waiting for him to say "Come in," I barged in and laid my five-page to-do list on his desk. I'd written the last item in red magic marker. *Benko! Keep him away from me!!!!*

Standing in front of Charlie, I raised myself up as tall as I could so he would have to sit back and see me staring down at him from the ceiling.

"Talk, Charlie," I said. "I'm trying to make this your best year yet, but how do I get everything done? This list. God and all his angels couldn't get it done in four weeks."

He scanned the list. "Good planning, Gen. You've become an excellent manager. Sit down. We can figure this out."

I hated it when Charlie patronized me with his management bullshit. I growled but he pretended he didn't notice.

"Seems you thought of everything. Now, add the amount of time you need for each step and chart it into your plan. It's not too bad. I have a list like that every week."

Yeah, right, Charlie, I thought. You sit around and make up lists and give them to the rest of us to do them for you.

"Why don't you hire a helper?" He surprised me with that, but it's what I wanted. "You need to be fresh for the TV shows."

When I glowered at him, he said, "Just kidding. I don't want you to overdo it. Get somebody good to take care of the admin stuff, the calls, reservations, minor things."

I sat on the corner of his desk to make sure he heard me. "I'll need a full-time helper, somebody who's good. I don't have time to train anybody."

"Try one of the office ladies. Sheryl? Maxine?

"Thanks, Charlie. It'll help. I can't guarantee perfection."

He held my hand in both of his. "Everything will be fine. It'll all work out."

When he said that, it sounded like an echo of Gianni assuring me about us against our impossible odds. Charlie dropped my hand and stood up. He almost pranced around to the front of the desk. His eyes shined, as if he were about to cry. I stood up to face him.

"By the way, Gen the Genius strikes again. Your to-do list just gave me an idea. Why don't we call our employee Chinese New Year part a *Tofu To-Do*? The Year of the Rooster!"

He crowed the four high notes of "Tofu To-Do. Tofu To-Do. Tofu To-Do." He laughed, whistling the notes over and over and we high-fived and low-fived. "Maybe I'll write a Tofu To-Do Tune," he said.

I couldn't believe him. He'd rope me into handling all the food and drink for the party, as usual. "Great idea. All I can say is you do the cooking. I won't have time."

"Nora will take care of it. All you do is supply the recipes and show up and enjoy yourself."

I felt relieved that he'd heard me and offered me some help. Given the realities of the upcoming month, I couldn't feel too comfortable, no matter what.

"By the way, what's up with Benko and you?"

"He's a creep. Because of him, we almost lost Wegmans as an account. My best customer!"

"Gen, you have to feel some responsibility for that."

"What? A mother's working her butt off for the company and a guy comes and takes her kid without telling her? I'm responsible? Don't make me any more pissed off than I am."

"Okay, okay. We've been over this. I understand how scared you were, but Benko said he was doing you a favor."

"Some favor. I could have him arrested-"

"Wait a minute-"

"Keep him away from me and my kid. If you don't..."

Charlie sat back on his desk. "I told him if he ever did something like that again, it would be the last thing he did as an AT employee. He was contrite. He said he was just trying to help you. I believe him."

Benko had Charlie as fooled as everyone else.

"We all have to work together, especially now when so much hinges on the next couple of months," Charlie said.

"When did I ever not pull my share of the load?"

"Gen, you're the most important person working here. Don't worry, please. If Benko annoys you, tell me and I'll take care of it. Give it a little time. Things can heal."

"Charlie, that's half of it. The worse half. I'm nervous about the media trip. "

"You'll have them eating tofu from your fingertips."

"I don't mean that. I mean Liam."

"Oh," Charlie said. "Yes. Anything we can do to make sure he's in good hands? Anything. We'll do it. He'll be totally fine. Hey, he can stay with us. I'll ask Nora."

I said I'd make arrangements for Liam, but I'd keep his offer in mind. Before I left his office, I told him if he wanted a miracle New Year sale, he had to carry some of my load. I must have come across as so desperate or angry that he agreed to handle some of the radio and newspaper interviews.

"Anything, Gen. We'll do this together."

Together to him meant he'd make big money and I'd get a paid comp time off. I wanted to resent Charlie, but at the bottom of my heart, I couldn't. I'm too forgiving. But I couldn't help myself. I felt bitter. I was not looking forward to all the travel and handling the inevitable tofu jokes with all the media.

At that moment, I resolved to give notice on Chinese New Year day. I'd give him four weeks, maybe stay on a few more to train the new person. Gone by lilac season.

It was my fault that Charlie expected miracles because I'd always given him way more than he asked for and now he demanded it. Not only that, but he planned for it. He spent so much money on this promotion that if we didn't do as well as he assumed the company might not be able to recover fully.

Later the afternoon after our meeting, Charlie buzzed me and asked if he could see me in my office. What now? "I've only got a few minutes," I said. "I just figured out the amount of time all these jobs will take. If I don't have any glitches, I'll be done in six months, a little late for New Year."

"I've got something to make it a little easier," he laughed. "I'll come to you. A two-minute meeting."

He sat down in my office's guest chair.

"Genevieve, you're better than the best salesman any company could have. After this is over, I'm sending you back to Cancun to recharge. The company will pay. I know you'll need a rest."

I heard Nora's urging behind Charlie's offer.

"Plus, you'll get a nice bonus this year."

At that point, I didn't care about the money. I just wanted to get the next month over with, but the vacation sounded incredible. Charlie must have read my mind or my face. A vacation in the sun. I needed it to carry me through the agony that work had turned into, then I'd have fresh energy to leave the company.

"Sounds beautiful, Charlie. A good vacation's just what I need." I fiddled with my pen and put the most elfin twinkles I could find in my eye. "One thing. Does it have to be Mexico?"

Charlie slapped my desk, laughing. "That's what I love about you, Gen," he said. "Always negotiating." He hugged me. "Go anywhere on the planet. No problem. Just come back."

I let myself sag against him.

"Go someplace hot and wet." He held me for a minute and raised himself on his tiptoes to kiss me on my forehead, like a father.

As soon as Charlie walked out of my office, I called Gianni. "Do you want to go to Saint Thomas or sailing in the Virgin Islands? He didn't miss a beat. "Let's go. When?"

"I surprised you, didn't I?"

"It's your late birthday present?"

"No, but Charlie's giving me a trip to someplace warm after the Chinese New Year. I'd hate to lounge on those beaches, all alone, wearing my iridescent green bikini."

"You'd better be all alone," he growled.

"There's one way you can make sure of that."

We laughed. Tears came to my eyes. I'd just agreed to be his mistress, for one glorious week, at least. I didn't want to talk about it, but sometime after our trip, we'd come to our new arrangement for the Year of the Rooster.

***

The first thing I had to do was to finish the new recipes for the promotion. Nora volunteered her gourmet kitchen as our recipe lab. She used it for her occasional party, otherwise she and Charlie and their kids could get by with a breakfast nook.

My kitchen was too small to spread around all the ingredients and dishes I'd need for the trial and error, splashing and spilling, recipe development thent required.

Work always energized me, so I was grateful the night of January second, when I shopped for two hours then hauled half a dozen grocery bags filled with enough wonton skins, Chinese herbs and spices, chicken and pork and beef, and vegetables to test a dozen new recipes.

I loved cooking on her restaurant-sized gas stove. She owned every kitchen implement and top-of-the-line brand machine known to modern woman. Mixing eggs and tofu and flour in her custom-thrown bowls gave me extra confidence in my baking. Best of all, leaning on a high-backed wood and leather-seated stool, I relaxed when I stirred and simmered in her designer copper and stainless steel pans and pots. I anticipated our intense but satisfying work, no phones, no problems, just me and food and her, and some laughs.

Nora had other things on her mind than the joys of dicing and stirring. We unloaded the groceries and set up the cutting boards and knives. I had at least three feet of ginger root that I would hack into half-inch slices. I laid out onions and garlic and the ginger and began peeling and chopping.

Nora stood beside me at the counter with a listless knife her hand and said. "Charlie's been acting so weird lately. Not just his dizziness, that's gone. You know, last summer when Benko called and said that a woman had died in the plant? Charlie thought it was you. He said if it had been you, he'd throw in the towel. He can't get along without you. None of us could."

I winced. Did she intuit my plans to leave?

"And now you and Benko are so estranged. Charlie says you're so mad at Benko you don't want him near you."

"You know why. You get it. Anybody who threatens your kid is no friend."

"I can't believe he meant it."

"He meant it. He did it to scare me."

"Why? He's a rough character, but why frighten you?"

"That's a long story. I'll tell you later. Right now, let's just chop and enjoy ourselves and forget about business."

Normally, Nora would stop everything and question me and sympathize and lead me on until I told her the whole story. Not that I usually held back on any subject, except Benko, she knew everything about Gianni. So, when she ignored my unwillingness to talk, I was relieved but surprised until she changed the subject.

Nora stared out the double bay window over the sink into the white January yard. "Charlie and I have been married for what, almost ten years? We had great sex for the first six, until after Rissi was born. Since then, it's pretty flat. But lately, y'know? He can't stop bugging me for it."

"Is that a bad thing?"

She ignored me. "He didn't want to touch me all last spring or summer. A lot of nights, we didn't even sleep together. Now, the more intense things have gotten, since Becky died, the Chief and all, the more he wants."

"It's a good tension reliever for men."

"Women, too," she laughed. "But I'm just not interested right now. It would be too much."

I peeled and diced the garlic while I listened. Sitting in a warm working kitchen with a friend makes you want to give up your deepest secrets and when you do, you feel so satisfied. Maybe because in a kitchen you feel safer than any other place in the house, or than in any other place in your life. I do.

Asking her to mix it with the ginger, I handed Nora the garlic and began sifting the won ton wrapper dough, listening, my nose now irritated by the bowl of chopped onions. I sniffled and let tears dribble down my cheeks.

She went on. "Charlie's not that bad a lover."

I rolled my eyes and arranged the bok choy and water chestnuts for their turns under the cleaver.

"It's just that I can't keep my mind on two lovers at once." "Nora. The painter is back?"

"No. Somebody else."

"Do tell." God, she and Charlie are just alike. If it's not one, it's the other.

"In therapy we'd been talking about the idea of an open marriage." Nora paused, expecting me to ask her who her lover was. When I didn't answer, she went on. "I guess I decided to try it out."

Then I asked. "Should I guess who it is?"

She grinned, then blushed, bracing her arms on the counter and closing her eyes, she said, "Benko."

I dropped my knife on the floor, jerking my foot out of the way just in time. "I can't believe it"

"'S true."

"How long?"

"Since last spring." She starting crying. "I wanna get out now, but it's so messy, y'know, how can I?" Fat tears rolled off her cheeks and splashed into the ginger she was slicing. She turned to me, lay her head against my breast and wept.

I circled around the end of the prep island and put my arms around her, clamping down hard on my anger. That son of a bitch, I thought. Lying asshole. I said to Nora, "All you have to do is stop. Right now. You can't see him anymore. Tell him to leave you alone. The only way."

"O my god. You don't understand. It's not that simple. He can cause a lot of trouble. I really fucked up. I shouldn't have ever looked at him a second time but he's so handsome. His voice melts me. I love the way he makes machines work, just by touching them."

What was it about the way he handles metal that turns women on?

"The first time we did it was last May, when Charlie sent him over to fix my bread baking machine. The way he touches me sometimes, like I'm a delicate flower. We have the same birthdays. October 10. Ten Ten. Same year. Like we know each other inside out like soul twins. He's so kind, usually...but I really blew it."

I raised my eyebrows.

Self-conscious, she chuckled. "No pun intended."

"Everybody makes a big mistake sometime," I said. "Just tell him you're done. It's all over. It was fun while it lasted but things have changed. You've said it before, every woman has."

Nora and I gave up on slicing and chopping. We sat down at the kitchen table. No doubt, Benko reveled in his duplicity. He'd conquered the two most important women in Charlie's life, and not only that, he probably slept with both of us on the same day, maybe more than once.

I knew I'd have to tell Nora sometime that she and I had been sleeping with Benko at the same time. A confusing mixture of anger and humor came over me. I felt like a fool. While I raged at Benko, I had to laugh at myself.

"But I'm afraid of him, y'know." Nora said.

"Don't be," I said. "He's a nobody. No friends, no money. If it weren't for American Tofu, he wouldn't even have a job. Tell him to leave you alone or he's out of work."

Nora's eyes narrowed. "You don't know him. He's crazy. You think what he did with Liam is bad. He'd try to destroy Charlie and me. He'd probably accuse us of murdering Becky."

Flabbergasted at that idea, I said, "Who'd believe him?"

Nora hung her head, dropping it onto her palms, lost in her feelings. "He's not always gentle," she said, "The first time he hurt me. I wouldn't do it without a rubber." She spoke into the table. "He wanted to feel the real me, y'know."

"What happened?"

"He forced me to. Grabbed my wrists and held me down. I fought. He ripped my pants off and fucked me. I fought him and then I gave in. It was the most amazing sex I ever had. I held on to him so tight and screamed and screamed. Afterwards he said he was sorry. All I could do was lay there in a daze. I didn't want him to know how much I loved it, y'know. Said he was only playing." She lifted her head. "He said he knew I'd like it a little rough, especially after being married to such a wimp. I got mad and said don't ever try that again and don't talk about Charlie. O my god, I was pissed." "Why didn't you stop then? That would have been smart."

"He apologized. Such a cuddly bear. A giant panda bear." She sighed. "He's got the biggest penis I ever imagined. I couldn't believe it would fit inside me, y'know. Must be a miracle, how it did. That thing's a log." She spread her hands to show me how long it was. "But I don't feel any more inside than I do with Charlie."

I didn't believe her but I said "Then you can get rid of him."

She didn't want to listen. "Another time he wanted to do it on my and Charlie's bed. You and Charlie were on some sales trip and the kids were staying with my mom. He practically dragged me into the bedroom by my hair. I yelled at him and he let me go. I thought he was following me into the living room and then he picked me up and threw me down on the bed."

"Nora, do you hear yourself? This guy's a beast."

"He's not. He's more like a teenage boy. He didn't really try to rape me that time. He never hit me or anything. He's passionate. He loves me." Her eyes pleaded with me to sympathize with her. "He's the most passionate man you can imagine."

"What if you told him no?"

"I don't know."

"He'd hurt you. You know he would."

Nora cried. "Gen, I'm afraid."

"You should be. What if Liam had an accident when Benko drove him to Canada? He scared me half to death. He's evil. Get rid of him. Right now." God help us, I prayed. Forgive us for all the stupid things we've done and don't let anybody get hurt. Please.

Nora said, "The worst thing? Now all he wants is to do it from behind. He makes me come to his house and strip while he sits on the couch. Then I have to kneel down in front of the TV, y'know, while he watches a movie. He puts his bottle on my back while he fucks me. It spills all over me and he licks it up. I feel like a pig."

I pulled her toward me. "Honey, this is serious. You've got to get out."

"I know. I don't know what to do."

"Sweetie, wake up. Stop seeing him. Why don't you come and stay with me and Liam for a while. Send Chuck and Rissi to your mom. She'll be happy to have them and they'll be safe from Benko. Maybe you should go out of town for a while."

Telling me her horrendous story had put her in some kind of a trance. Sniffling against my shoulder, she rambled on.

"I can't. You know that. Charlie would never let me go until I told him why. I'm not the only one in American Tofu either. Benko told me all the women in factory came on to him. He said he couldn't resist a couple of them. When he first came to Clement, he didn't know anyone. He just wanted to make friends and that's how he tried to do it. You have to admit he has great sex appeal."

"Did he tell you who else he slept with?" I hoped she didn't know about him and me.

"Well, he told me about a couple of them. I didn't want to hear, y'now. He told me I was the only American woman he could ever love."

Memories of his pledges to me, his passionate yearning gazes, his desperate lips that gnawed on mine like a starved child's, dropped to my stomach like scalding tea. Should I tell Nora? I had to...but not yet. "God. He laid it on thick."

"I got a phone call a couple of weeks ago. Bernice, the part-time night shift woman? She's done some ironing and house-cleaning for me, y'know? We're sort of friends. She called.

"'Don't mess with Benko,' she said."

"She told me she'd been his lover, he'd hurt her with his thing. Bernice is tiny. Not only that, she wouldn't do some things he wanted, so he hit her."

"Sounds like somebody better go to the cops."

"She said he was seeing Becky when she died."

"Shit."

"I asked Benko if it was true. He said yes, but not then. A couple of months before, she seduced him in the warehouse. He resisted but she reminded him of a Russian woman. When she hugged him and panted against his chest, he lost all willpower, y'know. He said he was sorry. He didn't want to cheat on me, it was only once. It's just, y'know, I was out of town and he felt so vulnerable and alone. He has a hard time with redheads."

My own red hair felt like flames rising from my guilty skull. "Did you fall for that crock of shit?" By now, I was fuming at

Nora and Benko, furious with myself. What did her comment about redheads imply?

"Gen, you don't know the half. Don't get mad at me. I finally told my therapist and she's helping me. After Bernice called, I stopped sleeping with him. Not because I don't want to—I still want to. I do. Nothing to do with him being a great guy or a great lover, y'know. I don't know why. Maybe I feel sorry for him, maybe it's only chemicals, maybe it does mean something great. If it wouldn't wreck everything, I'd sleep with him to-night, right now. I love his hand pressing on my stomach. It's better than a blanket."

"You've lost your mind, Nora. You can't be in love with him. He doesn't care about you. He just wants to fuck every woman who crosses his path. He's a predator. What's there to feel sorry for?"

"I can't help it. He has a sweet side, y'know. Did you know he was sexually abused by his uncles? His father wouldn't be-lieve him when he told him. I feel so sorry for him."

"Do you believe that?" I couldn't believe Nora was so gull-ible. "He'll say anything to get what he wants. You're smarter than this." "I believe him, Gen."

Her face went slack, adding years. Since Becky's death, Nora had begun to age. I saw her as an older sister, tortured by her effort to break out of her good girl role.

"He told me the details. It went on for years. They nearly killed him."

I didn't react, she continued. "You're right. He's put some kind of spell on me. Maybe some Russian magic. Last week he asked me for thirty thousand dollars for his mother in Russia. She needs heart surgery but only people with money get opera-tions in Russia. I almost wrote him a check. I have the money in my private account. Maybe I should have."

"I hope you're talking to your therapist about this." We clenched our hands together, our nails digging deeply into the pads of our fingers and palms.

She nodded yes. "Whenever I need to." She sighed. "He said, after Becky seduced him? She wanted a raise and a promotion. He didn't give it to her, y'know. She didn't work hard enough, he said. Then she threatened to tell Charlie Benko was sleeping with one of his workers. He gave her the raise so she would keep quiet. Sometime after she died, Benko snooped around her house, found her diary. He says the diary tells Becky was sleeping with Charlie right up to when she died."

"O my God!" I stood up, not totally surprised but now that it was in the open, at least among us, my heart went out to her. "I can't believe it. The Peyton Place of tofu. Everybody's sleeping with everybody?"

"I never thought Charlie would go through with 'open marriage,'" Nora said. "I let him say it because he needed to feel free. I didn't want him to leave our marriage because I controlled him and shut him down, like his mother did when he was a kid. He still resents her. But I was stupid and thinking too much of myself."

"Now Benko could stop all the bad publicity the diary would bring. All he has to do is keep it quiet or give it to us. If the press ever finds out? Can you imagine the headlines. 'The Boss and Me: Tofu Tigers in Bed!' It'd ruin us."

"Good god, Nora, Benko's grabbing you by the hair and fucking you like a mad dog. Does he sound like somebody who gives a shit about you? If he keeps things quiet, it's because he just wants to preserve his harem. You and every other woman in the company were his captive prey."

I changed the subject quickly before I got reckless and gave in to my anger at Benko and confessed my affair with him. I didn't want to hurt Nora any more, and if she knew, I was afraid she'd fall apart, so I asked, "Why did he wait so long to tell you about the book?"

"I asked him that and he said he was waiting for the right time." "The right time? Time for what?"

"I don't know. I think he wants a lot of money for it."

"Sure he does, that asshole." I grabbed her by the wrists and squeezed. "Nora, what on earth makes you think you can trust him at all?"

"I don't know. He said if anything ever did happen to Charlie? If the news got out about him and Becky, y'know? And Charlie went to jail or anything, Benko promised he'd help me run the company. He'd handle the workers and the factory and I could take care of the money part of the business. You'd be vice president of sales."

"Nora, he wants to take over everything."

"He's not that bad. Remember how much time he spent with Becky's kids after she died? He took them to the movies, stayed overnight a couple of times? He'd never hurt Liam, I'm sure, Gen. Deep down, y'know, he's a decent man. Just messed up about sex."

"I'll never trust Benko around my son again. I always wondered why he got involved with the MacDaniel kids. So he could snoop around her house? Or was it something else? The kids themselves?"

"That's stupid. Don't think that." Nora wandered over to the sink. She yanked the faucet on and swabbed at the counter with hard, skittering swipes. "He has his own kids in England. He misses them." I watched her, waiting out her thinking.

"Did Benko ever want to take your kids on a trip?"

Nora turned around. "What do you mean?"

"Face it, Nora. After what Benko did to me and Liam, he could do it to you. I'm worried about your kids."

"Ridiculous. He'd never touch a child."

"He kidnapped Liam."

"He brought him back. He told me he was just trying to help you."

"You're lost if you believe that. Benko's so clever he could convince the President to change parties."

Nora flopped down into the soft rocker next to the bay window. "You hate him, don't you?"

"I'm furious at what he did to you and to me and Liam." I paced around the kitchen. "If I were you, I wouldn't trust his production reports, either. I bet he's stealing from the company." As I spoke, I understood how thoroughly I feared him. "Nora, listen. You've got to make sure your kids are safe."

Her eyes glazed over as she tried to comprehend my anger and pleading. She lay her head back on the chair and rocked. "Maybe it did have something to do with his affair with her or the diary..."

Nora was smart enough to suspect Benko of the worst, yet she couldn't stop herself from defending him and putting herself and her kids in real danger.

I'd begun to give up on her, thinking I should tell her about my affair with Benko just to shock her awake when she said, "If I try to break up with Benko, he'll take the diary to the police and incriminate Charlie in Becky's death. I know he will. Charlie'd get charged with murder."

"God. If Benko did that, we're all finished. Did you ask Charlie if he slept with her?"

"I couldn't. He'd ask me where I got that idea. After Benko told me about the diary, Charlie came home in a rage. I asked him what happened and he told me everything."

"What?"

"Benko asked to meet him for lunch to talk about some production problem, but he really wanted to tell Charlie he had the diary and he knows about him and Becky."

"No wonder Charlie's acting weird."

"Charlie said he kept cool. He denied anything about Becky while he figured out how to handle Benko. Then, he said he couldn't help it, he asked Benko point blank how much he wanted for the diary. Benko grinned at him and said 'How much is worth?' Charlie said he wanted to slam Benko in the jaw but he forced himself into 'negotiation mode.'" Nora tipped a glass of water back and drained the whole thing.

"You gotta hand it to, Charlie," I said. "He's a wild man but he's consistent." I'd seen 'negotiation mode' plenty of times in sales meetings and he was so obvious in his insincerity. Not that sincerity would matter between him and Benko.

Nora put the glass down. "So Charlie says 'It's not worth anything.' And Benko says, 'I could get you in big trouble, Charlie. Be careful. I know you did it.' Then Charlie got up from the table and said, 'You show me this diary you claim you have and then we'll talk.' And Charlie comes home."

I couldn't believe Charlie would let Benko keep the diary, if it was true about him and Becky. If Benko had it. "Did you ask Charlie then if he'd been sleeping with Becky?"

"Yes. He admitted to it once or twice. A few times. Said he was drunk."

"Oh, no." Thank God I'd had the sense to start looking for a new job already.

Nora slumped back onto the chair, trying to burrow into the seam. She picked up a pillow and hugged it and rocked hard. "He couldn't have killed her. You know that. Charlie wouldn't do something like that. Besides, she was at her birthday party and he was with me that night, y'know..."

I was astounded at the thought that Charlie might have killed Becky. Impossible.

"If it ever went to court? I'd have to kill myself or something. I couldn't lie."

"What do you mean? Lie about what?" Nora could lie. She lied about her first lover, the painting teacher, she lied about Benko. "You can lie real well."

"The morning after the death? I found Charlie's clothes in the hamper. His pants and shirt were wet and muddy."

"So?"

"I asked him about it. He said he went out to the river for a few minutes while the kids were asleep. To meditate."

"Charlie meditates?"

"He goes out into nature and thinks about business, and things. Writes haiku, y'know."

"Still? What's the problem?"

"I don't know. He was lying to me about something. I'm afraid if the Chief or a lawyer asks me, I'll be the one to convict Charlie of something he didn't do. It's so fucked up, Gen."

I stood up and walked to the refrigerator and extracted a bottle of white wine from a loaded shelf. I filled two glasses and offered one to Nora. As I sipped mine, I said, "It's odd, but it's circumstantial. I don't see any relationship between Charlie's muddy clothes and Becky's death in the factory. Really. Think about it."

"You're right. But something's wrong."

"What's wrong is we know Charlie lied to everybody about him and Becky. But don't be ridiculous. Benko's a pathological liar, twisting your mind as bad as he's using your body. It's just as likely there is no diary. Does Charlie know you slept with Benko?"

"No way. That's the last thing I can tell Charlie. He's a mess. At home, all he does is sleep and complain. He's constantly plotting on ways to get the diary from Benko and shut him up."

We sat in silence, listening to the soup water boil. While she'd told her story, I'd forgotten where we were. Nora rose and with her head down and tears soaking her blouse front, she began cleaning up our half-finished recipe.

Her helplessness infected me with deep sadness for all of us. I wondered if we should just call Benko and tell him to go ahead, take the diary to the police, and let the chips fall where they may, get this over. I'd have to leave town sooner than I planned but Liam could handle withdrawing from school a few months early. We'd call off the Chinese New Year media tour and still have good enough sales. Charlie and Nora could hire the best lawyers in the state so they'd come out of this fine, a little dirtied, but they'd survive and so would the company.

As I heard myself tempted to give in to Benko, a criminal predatory rapist I'd had inside my body, willingly, enthusiastically, a few months ago, a sociopath, a conniving abuser of women, a kidnapper, I wondered how I could have fallen so low in my choice of men. I went from Gianni to Benko, a friend of the pope to the friend of the devil. A harsh laugh erupted from my chest.

Nora threw me a foul glance. "How can you laugh?"

She dragged around the kitchen, sponging the counter, the picture of a woman scorned, a woman beaten. She sniffled, wiped her nose on her apron, glanced at me, and smiled as if she understood that it was funny in a hopeless, tragic way. She walked in front of the refrigerator and stooped over to pick up ginger peelings from the floor. From over her bent back, Rissi's crayon drawing leapt at me off the refrigerator.

Ragged Christmas trees lit with bright yellow stars rode on the backs of horsey creatures whose heads sprouted antlers. Christmas tree bulbs decorated the borders of the drawing with red and green and orange patterns. I stared at the drawing. I breathed in and held it, letting a surge of anger rush from my nostrils down into my belly.

Listening to Nora's whole sad tale, I began to lose my temper. I was mad at Nora. Even madder at Charlie. I was enraged with Benko that he dared blackmail Nora and Charlie, everyone who worked in the company, so he could slam his cudgel dick whenever he wanted into a sweet woman whose mind he controlled in a way I knew too well.

"Nora, it's already 10:30. I'll finish up here, You go up to bed." "Charlie said he'd be home about two. He's driving in from Cleveland. I could help till then," she said.

"No. I'll take care of it. I can concentrate better if I'm alone. I'll be done by the time he's home. Only…I might not get everything cleaned up."

"No problem, sweetie. I'll call Sonia in the morning. She won't mind cleaning the kitchen. I pay her overtime."

Nora and I hugged goodnight, and she left the kitchen. I washed my hands, turned Nora's Pandora on to a Caribbean reggae station, and let the beat take me to work.

Scents of sautéing ginger and garlic rose around me and my knife danced with the leeks and chicken breasts. I sprinkled five spice powder into simmering sauce as if it was fairy dust transforming the world into a safe, happy, delicious place.

For the next three hours, I was all by myself, chopping, stirring, tasting, forgetting how lost we were, absorbing myself in the only dependable place I ever find peace, in the pure heaven of creating new dishes.

I left Nora's by 1:30, with three recipes finished and no Charlie in sight, thank goodness. I couldn't face him that night. He'd taste my gorgeous new dishes, mumble some compliment, then comment on how much money they'd make us.

Charlie was so predictable. If he only knew what was really going on.

Chapter Fourteen

Charlie

NOBLE GIFTS

*flinging white robes into
the lap of the valley,
winter hills shrug night off their shoulders*

I stopped taking business phone calls at home because I had to have peace someplace in my life. We got an unlisted home number for important calls about the kids or from her mother or our friends and we ran every call through voice mail. Nora and I changed our cell phone numbers and gave them out to a few key people.

One of the people I gave my new cell number to was Buhrman, another was Gladonov. Before either one tried to do something ridiculous to me, I wanted them to be able to give me plenty of warning. I never answered the phone when it rang but I checked the message immediately.

I thought Gladonov was my friend, a business friend but a friend, who I trusted enough to assign a critical piece of the operation making him as important to me as anyone. Somehow, I misinterpreted his management skills as a sign of his dedication to me.

If he was remotely a friend, even a loyal employee, he'd hand the diary over to me with the understanding that we were allies, together through the thick and thin, hanging in for the long run, building the business together, fighting back to back against the real enemies out to take American Tofu down. Instead, Gladonov showed his true colors by threatening me, and I was glad he did. Knowing where he stood and who he really was gave me an advantage, if I could only find it.

Except for necessary business meetings, Benko had kept to himself since he laid his diary scam on me. I expected him to offer it to me any time now for an exorbitant amount because he didn't really have any other play. He could take it to the police, but he obviously didn't care about being the hero.

Maybe Becky wrote something about him in the diary. Why not? He's her boss. If she did, he was either too worried or too clever to hand it over it to the police. Besides, the diary was circumstantial evidence. She obviously didn't write anything after she died. At worst, it would be embarrassing. Still, if it went public, I'd be mortified.

With relief, I realized that Gladonov had started to blaze a trail of possible guilt that my lawyers might be able to use to deflect suspicion from me, if they ever had to defend me. For a start, I'd have somebody research his immigration status.

Of course, if Gladonov furnished the diary to Buhrman, I'd deny I had anything to do with Becky. Women always fantasize about having affairs with men in power and this was one of those cases and besides, a diary was a pretty weak argument for conviction of a death.

I had to make sure Nora stayed away from Gladonov, too, in case he tried to intimidate her into offering too much money.

"I have it under control," I told her. "Gladonov's a complete liar. If he approaches you, don't say anything about my affair with Becky. Tell him you don't believe it and I denied it. I'll deny it until I see it written in her handwriting."

"I hope I can lie without him knowing. I'm a rotten liar," she said.

"For God's sake, Nora. We have to walk on eggshells around him until we get through the New Year. You know we need him to run the plant and we have to have the cash from the sales before we can do anything. I'll figure this out. I always do." Who was I bluffing? Not Nora.

I couldn't fire Gladonov for a lot of reasons. He had to handle the two week-long twenty-hour day production schedule coming up for our peak sales during the New Year. He must know that once the New Year push ended in February, I could fire him. Then, if things worked out the way I hoped, I would offer him a good severance package in exchange for the diary. If he didn't give it to me, he'd get nothing but the boot.

Blacklist him in New York State. He's made his fate.

***

I returned to my office from the gym one afternoon feeling unusually relaxed. My new personal trainer had started me on some stretching and breathing exercises that soothed me as much as a massage. I lounged on the office couch, studying the latest promising sales orders for the Year of the Rooster, when Meng called.

"Hello, Charlie," he said in a flat voice.

"Hello, Meng. It's been a little while. How are you?" The psychic infrared I've always had for bad news began blinking, sending a current to every fight and flight center in my brain.

"Good, Charlie. I want to talk for a minute."

"Sure. I have all the time you want." An icy tube of fear shot down the center of my body and my breathing went shallow.

"Charlie, starting March first, Meng Produce will stop doing business with American Tofu."

"What?" I doubled over my thighs with a pain in my stomach that felt like Meng had just kicked me. Our whole growth plans for the next year depended on Meng's opening of the national oriental markets. If we lost Meng, who knows who else would abandon us? I creaked my body upright and leaned against the soft couch back. My stomach ached.

"You can't. I mean, what did we do wrong, Meng? Give me a chance to work it out."

"It's already decided. I like you personally and don't want to hurt you. That's why we're waiting until after the Chinese New Year."

I should have paid more attention to him during the last month. The dizziness reduced my productivity to almost nothing.

He went on. "My farewell gift will be record sales for you during the month of February. I will pay everything I owe you as soon as I've shipped to my customers."

"But, Meng, we have the best product on the market. We can work on the price. Maybe we'll go to an Everyday Low Price for the Oriental market."

"Charlie, it's over."

"We could make you a private label. Your brand for your customers."

He paused, controlling the conversation. "Your tofu is fine. I don't need my own brand."

"What did we do...?" I waited in the silence. The phone dragged at my wrist like a twenty-pound weight.

"There are other reasons."

"What reasons? Who's taking over?" I wanted to shout at him. "You motherfucker. You just killed me!"

"I'm sorry," he said. "I don't want to discuss the reasons with you. The Quebec company will become my partner in tofu and other products."

"We had an agreement, Meng. The three-part agreement I worked out with Shu Ling? I haven't seen her for months."

My hand crawled across my desk top to the lucky pile of soybeans I kept in a raku pot. I picked up one bean and rolled it between my sweaty palms. The outer skin of the bean shriveled and slipped off the seed. I threw the naked bean as hard as I could across the room.

"It's all over, Charlie. I have appreciated our long and happy business relationship. Perhaps in the future we may do business again."

I'd remember that. "Shu Ling said you'd keep buying American Tofu." I let my voice drop before my obvious desperation humiliated me.

"Things have changed, Charlie. We can no longer abide by that agreement."

I didn't know what else to say. I lay back on my couch with one arm across my forehead, the other hand holding the phone to my ear. Thoughts and images of Taiwan reeled in my head. Nighttime Taipei spilling across my inner eye in oily neon rainbows...the Big Buddha's nostrils exhaling thick smoke... rats scuttling around the yard of the primitive tofu factory...the barbershop girl searching my crotch with her rubber glove...the carrion reek of the snake's blood rising up my nostrils...

Had I failed the test in Taiwan? I told him I'd consider importing for him. Or did Meng think Chen killed Becky and he was cutting his losses? Buhrman. He soured the whole thing. Did he sick the FBI on Meng? It had to be something out of my control. Should I play my ace and say something about the human organs? Or was it too late for that, too?

While my thoughts whirled, Meng waited silently on the other end of the line. In a minute I recovered enough composure to know if I wanted to preserve any positive relationship to protect myself, I had to retain face and to give him face.

Not only that, if Shu Ling had told me the truth, Meng was tied into powerful circles I could never hope to access. Circles that he could tighten around my neck if I wasn't careful.

I gave up trying to stop the inevitable. I couldn't do anything so I'd do nothing. Good old non-action: wu wei, the best martial arts move made the best business move. A graceful retreat was my best counter.

Standing up, I said, gagging at first, "Thank you for your gracious call, Meng." I got control of my throat. "All of us at American Tofu appreciate the business you've given us over the years. Your current decision is the best decision, I'm sure."

"You're welcome, Charlie." He sounded relieved.

I stiffened my voice with as much formality and objectivity as I could muster. "And thank you for staying with us through the Chinese New Year. That will help."

I quickly thought of a way to regain a little balance and salvage some pride. Almost casually, I offered him payment terms that he couldn't resist. "Pay us when you can, Meng. I'm never worried about payment from Meng Produce," I said. "Take as long as you wish to settle accounts."

He would understand the subtlety of my generosity: I determined the final form and the timing of his decision. But more important, I demonstrated that I was above business. My life, my world, would go on regardless of Meng's actions. Besides, it's a small world.

"Thank you, Charlie. Good luck." Did I hear a smile in his voice?

"Good luck to you, Meng. We'll probably see each other sometime. May the best man win." I couldn't resist challenging him. "Please tell Shu Ling hello from me." That was risky, I thought, but from now on it was simply Meng and Greer speaking man to man, so nothing rode on my keeping secret my friendship with Shu Ling. What the hell, this is how I wanted it, even though my knees were shaking.

"I will, Charlie. Good bye."

As soon as he hung up, I dialed Shu Ling. It rang twice before I put down the phone. She'd be no help now. Maybe she'd even been the reason Meng had gone with the Canadians.

If Meng didn't understand me, a unique individual with my own way of living life...like him...if he can't do business with somebody who has different values...who sees things his own way...an independent like me...eventually our relationship would have fallen apart anyway. It's better to get it done and let him bring in record sales.

Then, flash-I got it.

The Canadians will import the body parts. Good. Stay away from raw human kidneys, lungs, hearts.

Meng made a lot more money from kidneys and lungs than from tofu and bean sprouts. Shipping the organs through a Canadian customer would give Meng another layer of protection in case someone, maybe even Buhrman, stumbled onto something dicey, blew his cover.

I called Nora and Genevieve and asked them to come to my office. I broke the news and we all grumbled and stomped around and reassured each other. When they realized the dimensions of what had just happened to us, we all hugged. I made tea and we moped around my office until Genevieve came up with a great idea.

"Charlie, you should visit Gianni in person to tell him. He'll help, I'm sure. He'll sell to your old customers. They're used to American Tofu. Don't worry. This won't be as bad as you think. Thousands of refrigerators out there have to have their weekly supply of American Tofu. Don't be so emotional."

As usual, I followed her advice. That woman really knew how to sell.

***

Giordano had no time to see me at his office in New York before the end of January but he invited me to an early breakfast the next week at his estate in the Berkshires.

I'd suspected that Giordano was one of the richest men I knew, but I had no sense of the vastness of his wealth until I drove up to his estate that morning. His mansion perched on a hilltop, white and radiant among huge pines and bare-limbed oaks, above a snowy valley. I later learned that he farmed and forested several thousand acres in Massachusetts, Connecticut, and New York.

Seeing his riches, I felt curious, maybe even a little scornful, about his showing up for work every morning at Hunts Point. I'd be traveling Asia, windsurfing Hawaii waves, or strolling the streets of Rio if I were him. I'll never understand the rich.

Giordano's butler, a tall West Indian dressed in a purple velvet sweat suit, greeted me.

"Hello, Mr. Greer. My name is William, Mr. Giordano's assistant here at Lenox Farm. He asked me to beg your pardon for not being here, but he insists you stay for breakfast."

I almost turned around at that moment.

"Mr. Greer, please. Mr. Giordano apologizes. He instructed me to give you breakfast. He said he hoped you wouldn't be upset."

More than the butler, my stomach convinced me to stay. I might as well eat, no matter how disappointed I felt. In the foyer, he waited while I slipped out of my coat.

After hanging it up in a closet concealed behind a gold-framed floor-length mirror, William handed me an envelope. "I'm sure Mr. Giordano explains everything in the letter." He backed out of the foyer.

"I drive all night to meet with him, and he leaves me a note? He could have called me on my cell. My time's valuable." I ripped open the envelope.

First good friend Meng, now buddy Giordano. More good news? Keep singin' the blues. The note's gonna say he hired Genevieve away.

Numb, I sat on a mahogany bench to read. In his handwritten note, Giordano apologized profusely. He had to return to New York for an emergency breakfast meeting. He said he wished he'd had my cell phone number but he didn't want to wake up Genevieve to get it.

Considerate jerk, I thought. I read the rest of the note.

I read that and fell in love with Genevieve for the tenth time. She handled Giordano far better than I ever could. She was a better tofu sales person than I, no matter how she did it. She just did it, that's all I cared about. Besides, Giordano didn't need to meet me in person for me to achieve my goal of securing his ongoing commitment. My years of unrelenting service to his company proved to him how loyal I was and now, he proved his loyalty to me. This is why I love business.

His loyalty to Genevieve, Greer. That's what I hear.

We hit the bottom with Meng. Now we're on the way up.

Don't bet yet. Nothing's set.

William returned and invited me down a long, softly lit and paneled hallway into a bright dining room. He served me fresh-squeezed orange juice and espresso at an elegant setting on a long and heavy polished wooden table. Probably a Colonial antique, I thought. As William unloaded my breakfast from a filigreed silver tray inlaid with mother-of-pearl in the shape of a flock of chickens, I relaxed, Giordano's subtle humor surprised me, and I imagined owning a mansion like this when American Tofu became the largest tofu company in the Western world.

"Mr. Giordano had the chef prepare something special for you," William said. "He's quite well-known. Came to us from Il Pecadillo in Rome. I believe this is an original recipe. He told me to tell you he will send the recipe home with you if you like it. I'm sure you'll enjoy it."

"What is it?"

"Mr. Giordano said I was to surprise you. Do you prefer any particular music?"

My taste in music ran from U2 to Mozart, and not much else. Lately, I listened to hip hop, Becky's favorite music. I like the beat.

"What do you like, William?"

"We were listening to Cape Verdean tunes before you arrived."

"Sounds great. I've never heard that before. But, Mr. Giordano may have told you I like new things. I'm like your chef that way. Let's listen to it."

I devoured an exquisite meal of asparagus omelet with tofu bacon and fresh Italian bread. The tofu tasted far better than any bacon I remembered eating and the whole thing fit right into my new diet. While I chewed along to simple rhythms with bouncy singing and upbeat guitars, my eyes scanned the room, but the speakers were artfully hidden.

What else don't you see? Wealth has secrets, don't you agree?

Giordano's breakfast nook was a simple white room with a cathedral ceiling. From my chair, I looked out a bay window as the sky began to whiten. On each of the other walls hung a Norman Rockwell painting. Originals, too, I supposed.

The one I recognized showed a little boy and his puppy, sitting soaked and shivering next to a stream. A lump rose in my throat as I watched the boy and the dog gaze into each other's eyes like long-lost brothers. Maybe I'd get a dog for the kids.

Grateful that Giordano had been called away so I could enjoy a fantasy dukedom of my own, I lingered over a third cup of espresso and a snifter of the smoothest fruit brandy I'd ever tasted.

"Mr. Giordano wants you to take a bottle with you. It's from the *Giordano Collection*."

"I'd love to."

He changed the music to a throaty diva singing heart-wrenching blues. She suited my mood perfectly. Prolonging the moment of opulence and melancholy, I gazed into the broad valley outside as shadows slid back into the woods, leaving the valley floor clear and radiant.

Another ache formed in my throat as I realized that if I wanted my children and grandchildren to have even a sliver of the security and prosperity Giordano's family felt, I'd have to hang on to my company no matter what happened. I'd have to ride out any accusations, revelations, embarrassments, expenses, customer betrayals.

If the worst happens, I'll survive, I thought. No one will understand me, what I've gone through, who I really am. I'll be lonely, but so what else is new? I'll survive.

***

Groggy and road weary, I dragged myself into the office that afternoon with a brandy buzz. As I drove home, I'd sipped at Giordano's Collection, the smoothest, headiest liqueur I'd ever tasted. A different universe from anything Scotch, Irish, Russian. I wondered what other amazements Italy might have to offer.

I flipped on the lights in my office, planning to check my voice-mail and take a nap. A large FedEx package lay on my desk.

From Meng.

God, I thought. What now?

I peeled off the brown shipping paper. Inside a cardboard liner was a beautiful wooden box lacquered in black with scarlet designs in the style of imperial China. I held the box for several minutes, again recalling my trip to Taiwan, the tour through the bazaar, the temples, the girls. My fondness and desire for Shu Ling fluttered in my stomach like a promise of a wonderful vacation. I'd suffered strangeness and embarrassment during my association with Meng, but he'd brought excitement into my life like nobody else.

I lifted the painted lid with all the care an Imperial treasure deserved and, peeling back a wrapping of crushed red velvet, I saw what was inside. I immediately closed the lid.

What is he up to now? What did Shu Ling tell him about me? Did Buhrman get to him? Was he threatening me with something else?

I set the box on my desk, and made a cup of tea, lacing it with a big shot of my office brandy, not so fine as Giordano's—I'd save his for ultra-special times—but just the ticket. I'm not a drinking man so brandy at breakfast, brandy before lunch, brandy before dinner dulled my normal keen senses. My mind wandered. Maybe I should call Shu Ling...or Buhrman...or Genevieve...anything new out there in the stores? What was Nora up to?

Sipping tea in silence, I pondered the box. If I had to, I could probably sell it for a decent price to some sinophile, although I didn't really know any besides myself. Let it go on eBay if I had to.

It's a matter of pride. Hurry up. Look inside.

I raised the lid again and stared at the huge snake's head that lay cushioned in black velvet, its polished nose aimed at me with its toothy jaw propped half open and yellow glass eyes gleaming back, vengefully. It was as big as the anaconda whose blood I'd drunk and whose liver I'd chewed. Was this the same head that clenched mine between its jaws in old Taipei?

A metallic odor rose from the box, the same stench that plagued my nostrils for days after my visit to the snake house. As I bent closer, remembering the bizarre euphoria I'd felt when we all stood around slick with blood, guffawing and sipping snake blood cocktails, I noticed the snake's tongue curled around a rolled piece of paper.

I peeled the tongue back and, careful not to snag my fingers on teeth, I extracted the paper. It was a note in Meng's handwriting.

Charlie, I trust this will settle our accounts. Sincerely, MENG.

PS Big Man sends his regards. His business has never been so brisk. He's naming a new breed of snake after you. Charlie Yu. "Happy Charlie." Big Man told me next to the president of Taiwan, Charlie Greer is the funniest man he's ever met.

What did he mean? Did he think I made a fool of myself in Taipei? I bet they laugh their heads off every time they talk about Charlie, the clown from New York.

Meng was acting out of character. He could be covert, but never mysterious or, on the other hand, really forthcoming. I thought maybe the box itself was worth a few thousand dollars at most. I guessed that was about what Meng Produce still owed American Tofu for 30 days of past business, but the snake's head puzzled me. If I showed it around, I'd have to have a story to go with it. I'd never be able to tell the truth, but I'd have no trouble making something up. If I told it like it happened, nobody would believe me anyway.

I decided to make the best of it. I'd just call Meng and thank him, hoping he'd reveal his secret message. If not, at least I had a couple of new conversation pieces for my office.

I tugged the anaconda head gently, pulling it out of the box. Some of the velvet lining stuck to the scales so I dragged it out, too, intending to separate it once I laid the head on my desk. I gathered some flaky scales into a heap and unstuck the cloth from the snake. I picked up the case.

Eight thousand dollar bills lay on the bottom of the box. Oh, I thought, this is the settlement. Cute. I reached in to withdraw the nice little offering Meng had made. A deep pile of thousand dollar bills lay under each one of the top bills. I counted a pile—thirty nine bills. My palms began to sweat. I peeled away the layers of thousands, counted them all. My god. Three hundred twenty thousand dollars.

I peered at the face on the bill. William McKinley. Homely guy. What did he do to have his mug engraved on the thousand-dollar bill? Who cares? Meng gave me more than a year's profits on the business I used to do with him—in cash. Tax free? Maybe. It had to be. If I booked it, Buhrman could subpoena my records any time he wanted and learn way too much.

Jesus, now what did Meng want? Was he paying some kind of retribution because he thought Chen killed Becky and caused me all the pain? Was Meng feeling guilty that he'd given the future profits from my tofu business to the Canadians? I doubted that.

Don't be in such a rush. It's for the human organs. Give back the cash, or all you can do is shush.

Obviously, even though he'd brought me to the brink of ruin, Meng wasn't all bad. In spite of the fears that Shu Ling had planted in my heart, I saw, and decided to believe, that the Emperor of Hunts Point was acting as a consummate politician. He knew we'd meet on the fields of business for years to come and he didn't need me as an enemy. Besides, American Tofu was a perfect place to dump extra cash.

Three hundred twenty thousand was a nice sum, but not nearly enough to be a perfect bribe. Between Nora and me, we make almost that much in a good year. I felt the urge to call Meng and say, how about five hundred? If you want me to shut up, let's make it worth my while. How am I going to deposit this anyway? It'll take me six months to bury it in the business.

Of course, Meng was a master dealmaker. I couldn't call him now to talk about the gift. At best, I could thank him for the souvenir and the lovely antique box. In typical Meng fashion, he'd countered and upped the face-saving ritual I began when I told him to take his time paying his bill to AT, and he'd done it for a more than reasonable cost.

I'd keep quiet about the organs since, in actuality, transplants were common in modern medicine. It was only their source that the mainstream didn't approve of. Where would I be anyway if I did what middle-of-the-road people expected?

Meng knows you too well. He's sure you won't tell.

Once I accepted the money, I gave up any reason I had to seek revenge. Since it was significant but small, the amount felt almost like an enticement to respond with a more outrageous act. I had to hold off making any moves until I saw how things worked out with putting my business back on track through Giordano. This money was the sign I needed: once Becky's death was a closed case, everything would be normal.

IF, Greer. Remember the big IF here.

I thought about what to do with the money. I had enough to buy the diary from Gladonov with plenty left over. I could use a new car—my Jeep had nearly 200,000 miles on it. The Beemer was eight years old. One of the guys at the Y had bragged about his Lincoln LX. Best American car in history, he said. Mine would be a pure white cube of class: the new "TofuMobile."

Before I spent the money on myself, I thought I'd better bank some of the cash in the AT account to clean up the Meng Produce Bill. Then I realized a really odd thing. Meng had promised to do business with us through Chinese New Year. In fact, I had a huge tofu order from Meng Produce sitting on my desk that would mean even more profits.

I had to do some good with all this money, not just spend it on myself. I'd made a huge mistake, but with this money I could make up for it, at least a little.

I decided to put fifty thousand in the MacDaniel kids' fund, an anonymous cash donation. The local food bank always needed money. Another fifty thousand to them, mailed in cash from an anonymous donor in Rochester. I'd put a big chunk into my workers' year-end bonuses.

Maybe I should have been more suspicious of Meng, but when somebody loads your lap with even that much cash, no questions asked, you take it with a smile. Nobody needed to know about it. This was between Meng and me. In fact, it was only between me and me. "I and I," like those reggae singers say. Now I had cash—the unstoppable power source. Before long, I'd have the diary.

Finally, my luck was turning. Amazed, I bowed my head and imagined the Buddha's golden nose beaming at me. I whispered "Thank you."

Chuck, having fun? Don't get chill. We're far from done.

The End

Book Two

The Special Fruit Company

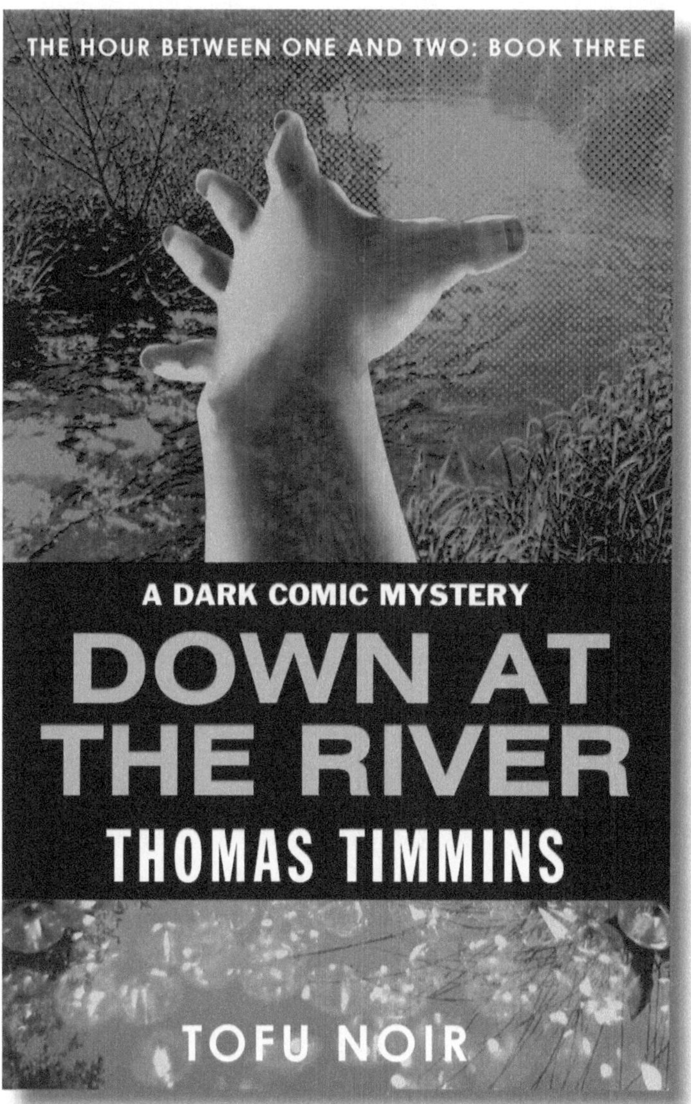

The story continues in
Book Three: Down at the River
by Thomas Timmins

Chapter One

Charlie

BLACKMAIL

we knew it was coming
but what could we do? he
thinks he's got me, ha!

A few minutes after I got back from lunch, Benko walked into my office without knocking. I spotted his shoe so I knew it was him before he came all the way in. He shut the door, and locked it behind him and I kept my head down, watching his reflection in the stainless steel base of my desk lamp. He stood leaning against the door until I finally said, "Yeah?"

"Production's going good, boss."

"Yeah, Benko, I know. That's your job. What do you want?"

"About that book? You got a good offer?"

I flashed a cold look at him, in his stained production whites, wearing short sleeves to show off his muscles, with a floppy net holding his hair off his forehead. I said, "Get that shit-eating grin off your face. I don't have a number for you because you don't have anything for me."

"You don't believe that. You know what I have and you need it. I give it to you. Cheap. Five hundred."

"Five hundred?" I said, half in shock. I thought he'd ask for ten thousand at least. "Go home right now. Get that book and bring it back and I'll have five crisp hundred dollar bills waiting, right here on the desk."

He laughed and laughed. Then he sat down on my couch and leaned back and crossed his legs. He spread his arms across the span of the couch and clenched his cucumber-sized fingers. A pulse rippled up his arms from his wrist to his biceps and disappeared under the sleeves.

"Thousand, boss. Five hundred thousand."

Flabbergasted, I sat still and closed my eyes.

"Cat got the tongue?" Gladonov said. "Five hundred by February."

He's playing a power card, but hang in, be hard.

"You're an idiot, Gladonov. You want to blackmail me, go ahead. I was thinking ten thousand was a high number."

He laughed again. "This is big company, boss. Make lot of tofu, lot of money. I see my workers' payroll every week. Figure office pay is pretty big. You, Nora, Genevieve, me, we make good pay. Right now, it's a record sales. You skim a little, hand it over to Russian friend. Save your ass."

"I'm not rich, Benko. Everything that comes in goes out the next day to pay bills. Anything extra goes to paying our people good wages, benefits, schooling."

"Bullshit. Your house, this factory. Record sales."

"Not bullshit. If you knew anything about business, you'd know we have assets, all mortgaged, and we don't have cash. I couldn't even get you fifty thousand from profits."

Benko leaned forward with his paws gripping his thighs and stared at the floor. As he pushed himself to his feet, he said, "Sounds like we're close," then he walked away. As he unlocked and opened the door, he said, "Four hundred, done deal. Like they say."

"Fuck you, Benko," I said.

"We talk later, Charlie."

He left my office and just before he closed the door, he shoved it open again.

"I like you, Charlie. Very nice wife. Nice kids, too. You don't want jail. It's bad place for soft guy. Tell you what? Make business deal: I run production for Chinese New Year, you make big money. Give me two-fifty at end of sale, another one, one-fifty in a month, I go. You stay out of jail. Deal?"

We were getting somewhere, and I figured he'd take two hundred, maybe one-seventy-five by the time we finished dealing. I might be able to handle one fifty if I hocked everything and tossed in some of Meng's boon, but at that moment, he disgusted me and I lost my temper. I snarled at him. "Fuck you. You're fired."

He grinned and came back into the office. "Be careful, Charlie. Nobody makes production hum like me."

"I'll appoint Jorge or, hell, Nancy can do everything you do. I'm not stupid, Gladonov. I have back-ups in place."

He knew I was bluffing.

"Sure. Tell me about it. Who knows electricity? Who keeps steam boiler up when electricity goes down?"

Only one guy in the whole company could keep the electricity running. The same guy who could shut it down and keep it off. If he didn't get what he wanted in cash, he'd take it some other way.

I stared at him until he said, "One last thing. You don't want the diary, you know who does. I don't mean Nora."

He closed the door quietly, whistling as he went down the long hall toward production.

***

I called Nora and told her to take the kids to her mom's. I'd be home in twenty minutes. We had to talk.

As soon as I came in the door, Nora said, "What happened, Charlie?"

"Benko," I growled, taking off my coat. I was fuming.

"Benko? What did he do? What did he tell you?"

"He didn't do anything, yet. It's what he plans to do. He wants five hundred thousand dollars or he gives the diary to the Chief. He might sabotage the plant, too."

"Five hundred thousand? Where does he think we'll get that?" Nora's voice trembled.

"I'll tell you when I get home. Take the kids to your mom's. I'm almost finished here and I'm out the door."

***

An ugly sky squatted on the tops of the house and the bare sycamore and oak bordering our property. At least the low-pressure system raised the temperature above freezing for the first time in a month. All of upstate New York could get a foot of wet snow during the night.

Nora was in the kitchen brewing coffee when I came in. Without speaking, I hung up my coat and hat and walked over to her. When I hugged her, trying to establish our togetherness against Benko, she didn't stop shivering. It was infectious and shudders ran through me, too. I turned the thermostat up to eighty.

We carried our cups into the living room where Nora had built a fire in the fireplace. I spiked my coffee with a shot of Maker's Mark and stared into the flames. Nora sat on the edge of her chair, tapping her heel on the maple floor. I inhaled the sweet peppery fragrance of the burning birch and turned around. She was still shaking.

Nora stood up and crossed the room to the liquor cabinet. "I better join you for this one." She poured herself a splash of the bourbon in a glass. "Sit down, Charlie. You're making me way too nervous standing there."

"I don't know if I can." I sat down and got right back up. "I can't talk sitting down."

Nora shrugged and raised her glass to me. "Whatever. Walk. Talk. Tell me what's going on."

"He sent an email asking for a meeting. I knew what it was about. Let him come, I thought. I told him to see me in my office after lunch—my turf, my time."

I told her the whole story, ending with his threat to disable the factory if I didn't give him the ransom.

"He has me by both balls, now. The plant and the Chief."

Nora ignored my comment and said, "Is it true? Is he the only one who can handle the electricity?"

I snapped back. "Yes, goddam it. It's complex. We're too small to afford two skilled electricians on staff."

"I wasn't accusing you."

"Benko meant if I fired him, he'd sabotage the plant, cut the electricity."

"He wouldn't."

"What world do you live in?" For all her numbers and business acumen, Nora could be so naive about people.

"I'll talk to him," she said, pouring herself another finger of whiskey. Tossing a log onto the fire and settling herself on a footstool in front of the fireplace, she stared into the orange blaze. "He'll listen to reason. He and I have always had good communications."

"Stay away from him. I don't trust him. If he comes near you, call me. I'll handle Gladonov."

I hadn't told her about the cash Meng sent me, and before I dipped into it to ransom the diary, I'd try waiting Gladonov out. I'd had twenty years of negotiating experience and, unless he resorted to violence, I was sure I could beat him down to a reasonable fee. I might have to pay, but I'd pay as little as I could.

As I started toward the liquor cabinet, Nora rose and put her arm around my waist and lay her head on my shoulder. Her breath smelled sweet with bourbon.

"We'll figure it out, Charlie."

"It's a business battle, Nora. We win this one, we're home free." I lifted my arm over her head and dropped it around her, pulling her gently to me.

After a minute, she said, "Hey, look out the window. It's started."

In the west, the sky had turned blue but over our house the clouds had opened. Fat snowflakes sputtered down with deceptive delicacy.

I said, "I bet we'll get a foot by dawn."

With her ear still pressed against my chest, over my heart, she said, "Let's go for a walk before it gets dark."

"What about the kids?" I said, not wanting to leave them stranded during a blizzard, even with grandma.

"We'll walk first, then we'll pick them up, come home and roast marshmallows."

"God, Nora. I don't know how you can be so playful at a time like this."

"Don't worry, Charlie. I'm not feeling playful. This is survival. Hunker down with family on a snowy night. That's common sense."

***

I checked the thermometer outside the kitchen window. The temperature had dropped to twenty-three, perfect for an all night snowstorm. I retrieved Nora's and my down jackets and brought them to where she waited.

"You know, honey. It's strange," I said. "I feel good, well, not exactly good, but mentally clear. Benko started the bidding, laid out his hand, and said, come on, Charlie, your bet. Now I know about what he wants and his position, we have a good chance of working this out."

Nora sat down on the stool she kept by the serving island in the kitchen.

"Hey, let's go," I said, tossing her a coat. "Before it gets too slippery out."

She caught the coat and lay it on the island. "Take your coat off, Charlie. Sit down."

"What? I thought you wanted to go walking? We can figure out a plan to get the diary."

"Not yet. You said you knew a lot more about him? And that improved our odds?"

"Of course." Nora had become her serious and distant self again. "Don't tell me you know something else, something I don't." I sat down and bounced back up, searching for my glass.

When I couldn't find it, I went over to the island and sat on the stool across from her. "So?"

Nora raised her eyes to the ceiling, then, with her chin in her hand, she glanced around the room.

"You're making me nervous now, Nora. What?"

"All right," she said, her brown eyes liquid and sad. "You have to know this."

My heart started thumping in my ears. I was afraid of what she would say.

"I'm really sorry, Charlie. You know how I didn't come down on you when you told me you slept with Becky? I kind of accepted it and said let's make the best of it?"

"Yeah. By then, what else could we do? Benko had the diary." "And I'm one hundred per cent supporting you in the investigation?"

Uhoh, here it comes. Fee fi fo fum, don't get yourself bummed.

"Why are you saying this?"

"Remember, I never tried to hurt you. I made a mistake but it wasn't because I had bad feelings about you."

"What mistake?"

"I slept with Benko."

"You slept with Benko?"

"I'm sorry. Yes."

Could it be any worse? Only riding in the back of a hearse.

My throat clutched and I gagged. Sputtering, I groaned, "How could you? How could you? Gladonov?" She tried to take my hand but I jerked it away and slammed my palm into the refrigerator door.

Nora called after me, as if I were already out of the house. "I couldn't help it, Charlie. You weren't interested in me. He paid attention to me. I wanted a summertime fling, that's all. You had one. Yours ended in total disaster."

How could I deny that? I didn't try. Instead, I shouted, "The lowest snake in the grass is fucking my wife. How the fuck could you do that with that criminal?"

Nora stayed quiet, sitting at the counter. She'd laid the coat on her lap and was playing with the fur collar while I ranted and raved.

I felt about an inch high but I wouldn't let her see that. "Where did you fuck him? Here? Right here on that fabulous oak island I had hand-made for you for five thousand dollars?"

Nora stood up. "Stop it, Charlie."

"Sure, I know where you fucked him. Right in front of our romantic fireplace?"

"Stop acting like a two year old. I'm sorry. It was a big mistake. It's over. It's been over."

I swung my arms and picked up my coat and threw it as hard as I could at the cupboards. Then I faced her and growled, "I bet you did it on our bed."

"No, never here," Nora said. "We only did it a few times. Like you and Becky."

The words I'd used to minimize my affair with Becky flew out of Nora's mouth and slapped me across my jaw.

I recoiled. "Oh. Like me and Becky ... like me and her."

No surprise. It's the old new age. You got it: open marriage.

I laughed, not a funny laugh, but a hard, sad laugh. "Nora, you and me," I said. "A couple of losers. We should never have got married. No wonder you wanted that open marriage crap."

"You're right. I know. But we are married and we both screwed up big time. I'm sorry. You're sorry. What else can we do?"

"All the time we're in therapy you're dicking Gladonov. Such a liar." She had me completely fooled. What's worse, Gladonov knew I didn't know about him and Nora. No wonder he smirked at me when he asked for half a million dollars. He'd already conned me out of something far more valuable.

Nora came across the kitchen to within a few feet of me, ready to don boxing gloves, if I wanted to, though she knew I'd never strike her.

She said, "Don't start that hypocrisy thing, Mr. Hypocrite. I was stupid, I admit it. But you were in therapy with me when you were fucking your employee. What's so honest about that?"

Our anger escalated and we started shouting until Nora walked out to the back yard and stood in the twilight, hugging herself. I watched her while I cooled off.

She said it was over with Benko. She wasn't leaving me for him. We were still a team. I wanted to keep it that way, at least until we got the diary. We'd get Benko gone and then we could sort out our lives.

I picked up her coat and slid down the back steps to bring it to her. I brushed the snow off her hair and sweater and settled the coat on her shoulders. I snugged it closed around her and said, "Look at us. What a strange pair."

For the first time, she started crying. I pulled her against me and said, "We can get through this somehow, Nora. We've made it this far. But it's gonna cost us."

"I know," she said. "We have to pay Benko now, don't we?" "Pronto," I said. "The only question is, how much more?"

The author

Thomas Timmins has published and performed his poetry and short fiction in person and in print across the U.S. and on the internet. He founded Fractals, a literary tabloid, cofounded and ran Poets & Players, a performance venue, developed and taught writing and coaching programs for inmates, published commercial writing, and founded and managed small businesses ranging from soyfoods to ice cream to telephone fundraising to biological pest control to a video game start-up to energy efficiency retrofits and a media company.

www.thomastimmins.com